TELL ME A STORY, TELL ME THE TRUTH

*To Andrew,
So happy to share
my stories with you.*

Tell Me a Story, Tell Me the Truth

GINA ROITMAN

Second Story Press

Library and Archives Canada Cataloguing in Publication

Roitman, Gina, 1948-

Tell me a story, tell me the truth / by Gina Roitman.

ISBN 978-1-897187-53-1

I. Title.

PS8635.O443T45 2008   C813'.6   C2008-905386-9

Copyright © 2008 by Gina Roitman
Edited by Carolyn Jackson
Designed by Melissa Kaita

Printed and bound in Canada

Second Story Press gratefully acknowledges the support of the Ontario Arts Council and the Canada Council for the Arts for our publishing program. We acknowledge the financial support of the Government of Canada through the Book Publishing Industry Development Program.

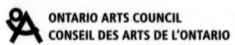 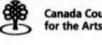

Published by
SECOND STORY PRESS
20 Maud Street, Suite 401
Toronto, ON M5V 2M5
www.secondstorypress.ca

*In memory of my late parents,
Sula Kluger and Benzion Miedwiecki,
whose words guide me still.*

CONTENTS

1	Introduction
3	An Imperfect Child
25	A Whole Heart
33	Mr. Greene and the Studebaker
69	Remember My Words
85	Hebrew Lessons
117	Tateh and the Angel of Death
129	Missing in Action
147	Pesach en Provence

"Everything is connected. We're all part of the same thing. So history became much more important for me than I thought. Because it connects, I cannot cut it off. I'm fascinated how I came to be what I am."

—M.G. *Vassanji*

INTRODUCTION

We argued all the time, my mother and I.

I was unruly, independent, and stubborn as a child and my mother was unyielding, single-minded, and determined to mold me to her will. She would tell me what I must do, and I would deliberately do the opposite. That was the motif of our relationship for close to three decades. I willfully ignored her admonishments about the dire peril she saw lurking around every corner of my life. And I tested her determination to make me in her image of perfection, to live the life she had been denied by poverty and war.

Exhausted, she would end battles with *"You will remember my words."*

My mother died at sixty-three; I was twenty-eight. I am now more than double that.

I don't recall when it started, but slowly, not too many years after her death, I realized that every day, something my mother had said, some expression of hers, would somehow materialize in a conversation.

She crops up in my stories—her words, her expressions. They often steal the limelight from other characters. Finally, I have acquiesced and gratefully give my mother *kouvet*, respect, for her shrewd observations of life and people. When I'm in doubt, she is still the strongest voice in my head.

—Gina Roitman

AN IMPERFECT CHILD

I WAS BORN with my nose out of joint. I don't mean I arrived ill-tempered; in fact, some people find me relentlessly cheerful and feel they have to work hard to prove to me that the world is a perilous place. No, I mean I was born with a deviated septum, a legacy from my mother, from whom I also inherited other more appealing attributes, but those didn't develop until later.

I sometimes wondered if my mother might have been disturbed by what was then a tiny deviation in my nose. Did she find me imperfect? Probably not. Maybe she was comforted that we shared this physical feature, telling herself or my father, "Look how much we are alike."

I was, in fact, a miracle. My mother had been told she would never bear children again, yet there I was, ten months after her marriage to my father, a big baby girl, weighing in at a whopping twelve pounds, fourteen ounces. And in such a hurry to get on with life, I popped out after only twenty minutes of labor. Not bad for a woman who had almost died of malnutrition four years earlier. Anyway, I had ten fingers and ten toes and was perfect, absolutely perfect—except for that crooked bone in my nose.

My parents met after the war in Pocking, a refugee camp in Germany where they were introduced in the hope that they would like each other well enough to marry. They didn't actually have to love each other. The war was over, life could now go on. Life meant children and children meant marriage. My parents believed that they would learn to love each other later. They married there, in the camp, and there I was born. My mother explained this all to me on the day I became a woman at the age of eleven, right after she said no, I wasn't going to bleed to death and then spelled out the facts of life. In a level voice—more level than what I was accustomed to—my mother explained that both she and my father had lost their families in the war. First her husband had died and then her three-year-old son. My father had a wife and three children before the war. All four died in Auschwitz. Drora, the eldest, would have been old enough to be my mother, all things being equal. But all things aren't equal, are they? Why else would I have to make a quantum leap from being a tomboy to a full-blown woman just because of a little blood? And then my mother said, that because I had become a woman, I would have to be responsible and understanding. I did think to ask her if she and my father now loved each other. She said they were still learning. At eleven, that was that. I kissed my childhood good-bye.

Aside from a deviated septum, I was also born with an *alteh kop*, an "old head." That actually sounds much better in Yiddish, my mother tongue. It meant I was someone who knew too much or was wise beyond my years. I may have earned that epithet early on by the little gestures of comfort I would offer my mother, mimicking the actions I had observed in other mothers. Sometimes when she began to cry for no apparent reason, I would put my arms around her as far as they would reach, and I would kiss her tears until they stopped. In those times, she would pull me fiercely to her chest and scan my face as if searching for someone familiar. It was then she would call me *Leahleh, meine alteh kop*. But if I crossed her, my mother could hurl words like a knife-thrower in the circus, not meaning to stab me, just to pin me to the wall and put on a good show. When angry, she slipped easily from Yiddish to Polish to Russian. She had a gift for languages that I did not inherit. But the words I heard most often were not addressed to me but to God. When I displeased her, my mother would raise her eyes heavenward and demand, "I survived Hitler for this?"

Long before I understood who he was, Hitler played a major role in my childhood. Sometimes I imagined my mother's world was split into two: the past where Hitler was the source of all her misery; and the present where I was. I didn't always understand the horror of the stories my mother relayed, maybe because of the way she would tell them. They came at odd times, like the one she told me when I was four and wouldn't eat my lunch.

She and her sister, Baileh, and her five-year-old niece, Chana, were running from the Germans in a farmer's field. The day was cold and rainy, and her niece was whimpering in terror as they ran. There was a barn in the distance. My mother, unencumbered, reached the barn first and clambered up into the loft, where she buried herself beneath the hay. But her sister and niece had fallen behind. The soldiers shot Baileh as she ran. She toppled over Chana, who was screaming in terror. Frozen with panic, my mother watched, her face pressed against the cracks between the planks of wood, as the soldiers lifted her young niece and tossed her in the air just a few feet below her hiding place. Her niece disappeared and the wall shook. Dust rose from the wood and flew into the air around her. My mother saw her niece again, like a broken doll, lifted from the ground and thrown into the air a second time. Once more the wall shook and once again, dust flew into the air, settling on my mother's head and on the hands that she had clamped over her mouth to keep from crying out. By the time my mother had finished the story, I had finished my lunch. Although she never told it again, I never forgot a word.

My mother had survived, the only one of five sisters, and like most survivors, never ceased questioning why. She had not been the prettiest or the smartest, not even the most talented. She certainly hadn't married well, choosing to fall in love with a handsome communist. She took pride in telling me she had been the practical one, the one who always made certain that there was a chicken for her parents' *Shabbos* dinner. By the time she was seventeen, she was running her brother-in-law's sweater factory; she was always good with her hands. That I did get from her. Maybe, being the middle child, my mother survived because she had to fight for her place in the family.

Somehow my mother had salvaged a number of photos. They were kept in a soft, navy leather pouch on the top shelf of her closet, next to a pair of blue suede platform sandals from the Forties that I finally convinced her to throw out six months before they came back into fashion. She hated throwing anything away, and never forgave me for giving her such bad advice.

With the intensity that a child gives to a jigsaw puzzle, I would scrutinize these dog-eared remnants of another world. There were three photos of Baileh, her eldest sister, one with Chana in her arms, but none of her other sisters or of her parents. My grandfather was strictly orthodox and didn't believe in photography. He was a bookbinder, but I got my love of books from my father.

Many were photos taken with her friends Oskar and Lipke, whose big toothy grins were a sharp contrast to my mother's sullen smiles, parsimoniously dispensed for the camera. Sometimes they would be standing among a large gathering of their comrades from Habonim, the Zionist organization they all belonged to. Of course, these photos included her fiancé, David, whom she married before leaving Krakow and heading east to Uzbekistan at the outbreak of the war. She had several photos of, and with, him. It would never occur to her to hide these from my father.

David was strikingly handsome, with a lean body, warm deep-set eyes and thick, dark hair with a Superman-like cowlick that fell over a corner of his high forehead. There were several photos of them together, one of them sitting on a split-rail fence and another where they were standing in a shallow stream, wearing those funny loose bathing suits of the Thirties that outlined more than they hid. You could see that my mother was well-endowed, with a small waist and lovely legs, but not pretty. Their arms are around each other's waists and my mother is gazing directly into the camera, her lips turned up in a smile that had not reached her eyes. She appeared to be looking right through the photographer.

One photo of my mother at seventeen terrified me because I worried I might look like that when I grew up. It wasn't that she was unattractive just that . . . well, her face was blank, like a sheet of paper before a letter is written—no characters with interesting lines and curves. But the war would transform her face. I know this is a terrible thing to say, but misery made my mother a pretty woman.

Then there were the post-war photos taken in the *lager*, the Displaced Persons camp, outside Passau in the southeast corner of Germany, near the Czech border. It was from there that we finally immigrated to Montréal, when I was eighteen months old. In one photo, taken in the lager, my mother is walking arm in arm with my father down a broad avenue of the town. The camera has caught her in mid-step. Her shapely leg is out, as if anxious to move forward into some promising future. She looks almost happy. There's another of her alone, visibly pregnant with me. She's wearing a mannish hat, jauntily pulled down over her brow, and a stylish pinstripe suit, sewn by my father. It had a long, tailored jacket that would still be in vogue today. There is a calm, peaceful expression in her eyes and a small, comfortable smile on her full lips. My favorite photo, however, was the one taken a few months before my first birthday. I am being held aloft, wedged between my beaming parents and superimposed beneath in Hebrew are the words, *Shana Tova*—Happy New Year. I suppose as young as I was, I believed totally in my ability to make my parents happy by my mere existence. Later I would come to believe that I filled the vacuum the war had created in my mother's life, replacing what she had lost. She had so often said that I was everyone in the world for her; there was no reason for me to believe otherwise.

The first home I remember clearly is an apartment building on Lajoie, a wide street with stately trees growing straight and tall on either side, their branches reaching across the road in friendship. These mature maples marked the sweet seasons of my youth. The building was a three-story, square structure, with two small concrete steps leading into a marbled vestibule. It was bordered on the right by Main Lane that ran for five blocks from the grounds of the Catholic church one street above Lajoie all the way down to Bernard Avenue in the other direction. On Bernard, around the corner to the left of the lane was Robil's Ice Cream Parlor, the barbershop, and National Variety Store, presided over by the genial Louis who had two black Betty Boop curls plastered on either side of his wide, thinning scalp. At the corner of Outremont Boulevard stood the pharmacy we didn't frequent. We would go to Clayman's further down the street because the owner spoke Yiddish.

From the building to the lane, from the lane to the corner pharmacy and from there, down Outremont to the corner of Lajoie, these were the boundaries of my young world. And in the center, behind our apartment building, branching from Main Lane was Middle Lane that ran parallel to Lajoie. This was the hub of my realm. I knew every inch of that turf, and years later would recall it in my mind's eye, as if in a scene from *West Side Story*. Me, I was a Jet, leading my own small gang.

Inside the building, past the vestibule with its metal mailboxes, neat names, and round black buzzers, was a glass door framed in rich, varnished oak that could not be opened unless you were buzzed in or had a brass key. An elongated star pattern was blazed into the glass. Ruthie Williamson once said it looked like the Star of Bethlehem that had heralded the birth of the baby Jesus. A flight of steps was flanked by a marble banister, polished smooth and shiny by years of hands gripping it firmly and by the many times I would slide down it in a cheerful hurry to get outside. There were only four apartments per floor, two in the front and two in the back. Ours was one of the two facing the back, Number 8, on the left-hand side, right at the top of the stairs. Mrs. Crotty, a widow with gentle green eyes and a tolerance for noisy little girls, lived on the right with her black-and-white Boston terrier, Nipper. I asked my mother if we could get a dog too, but she said we couldn't afford any animals and that I was animal enough for any household. Then she kissed me on the head so I would know that she had not meant it unkindly.

On the other side of the varnished wooden door was our sparsely furnished, four-room apartment. From the hall, you could see straight through the double parlor to the back door balcony. The first half of the parlor served as our living room and was dominated by a big wine-colored sofa in that scratchy fabric that looked like chenille but is much harsher on your naked legs when you sit on it too long in summer. The floors were bare and the walls without pictures or prints. My parents had bought the sofa, a matching wing-tip chair in pearl gray, a square dining room table without chairs that stood tucked in a corner, and their bedroom suite, all of it second-hand, from a peddler. Every Friday around four, the peddler, who smelled of onions, would knock on the door to collect that week's payment. Often my mother would have me answer because her hands were full of chicken gizzards. I would do so with some reluctance, as the peddler, upon seeing me half hiding behind the door, would gleefully reach out to give my cheek a mighty pinch, as if this too was something that we owed him.

Two enlarged photos decorated my parent's bedroom. On the high-boy dresser where my father kept his clothes, sat a tinted photo of me at six months old, sitting up and looking as squat and solid as one of those punching bags you can't knock down. My fat little fist is holding a drawstring knitted into my dress, which the photographer had tinted dusty rose. My eyes are deep blue but the photographer had placed a greenish wash over my scalp, so I loathed that photo. Next to it stood a tinted photo of my father's mother, the only photograph of his dead family he possessed. In it, my grandmother's hair is black, pulled into such a fierce knot at the back of her neck that I imagined there was no slack available for her to turn the thin line of her pink lips into a smile. She had dark eyes sunken deep beneath a prominent brow that looked out at the world with a particular ferociousness.

The room I shared with my brother, David, was to the left of my parent's "bedroom" behind the kitchen. There was a four-drawer dresser, my bed, and, once my brother outgrew his crib, a dull, greenish-gray sofa-bed, the kind that had a spring, allowing the back to lie down flat. This became David's bed at night. Our feather-down comforters, brought in a big wicker trunk from Germany, were kept in the storage compartment beneath the seat. That coffin-like space was also where I would convince my brother to hide, promising him I would let him out as soon as he knocked twice. I never did, but he fell for that over and over again, just happy to have me all to himself. Once, I went to the bathroom and altogether forgot that my brother had crawled inside. My mother, shaking out the sheets of her bed, heard his muffled cries, and pulled him out shrieking and purple in the face. I escaped through the front door, knowing I would get a smack if she caught me. Escape sometimes saved me from a beating.

Early on, I knew that my mother was different from the other mothers in the building. For one thing, she looked much older. Her hair was dark brown with streaks of silver threading through and cut short, giving her lined face a somber appearance except when she smiled. This she did not do often enough. Three other girls my age lived in the apartment building on the ground floor. Ruthie Williamson, an only child, was blond and blue-eyed, with a little turned-up nose. Her mother always smelled of freshly baked cookies. For some reason, I imagined that our new queen, Elizabeth, must smell just like Mrs. Williamson. Maybe because they both wore their hair the same way and Mrs. Williamson was always smiling even when she was displeased. I envied Ruthie, who had no little brother tagging after her everywhere. Instead she had a budgie called Tweetie, parties on Halloween, Christmas, and her birthday, and best of all, a room of her own.

Terri Stroll was a year older than me, but much smaller, with dark, straight hair and brown eyes that were always full of mischief. She had a teenage sister, Joyce, who wore white bobby sox and her hair in a ponytail. Terri's mother, who insisted I call her Ida, was pretty and petite. She smoked cigarettes that she would tap loudly on the closed pack before lighting. Once lit, she would remove a stray piece of tobacco from the tip of her tongue with her thumb and middle finger, closing one eye to avoid the smoke. She loved to have me comb her hair. She was always making jokes, at which she laughed raucously. I didn't understand them, but I loved to laugh along with her. Terri's apartment was one of my favorite places to hang out, especially after I was forbidden to play with Monique, the janitor's daughter, who spoke to me in French. Even though I replied in Yiddish, she had become my first friend. I used to love watching her father, Mr. Portuguese, shovel the coal into the bin when it came down the chute through a hatch that faced out onto the lane. I also loved to sit in her big kitchen with its foreign smell, which my mother said was probably pork. We never ate pork, it was *treyf*. Mr. Portuguese always lined up his bottles of beer against the kitchen walls, starting at the right side of the doorjamb. When they had ranged all the way around the room, arriving at the other side of the door, Monique and I would be given the job of filling the wooden crate that he would then take in for a refund and a new case of beer. One day after an afternoon with Monique, my mother discovered a louse in my hair and that was the end of my visits to the basement apartment, although Monique and I still secretly played together in the furnace room next to the coal bin until we both started school. After that we seemed to lose our ability to communicate. Monique never learned English and I quickly forgot whatever French she had taught me.

My friends rarely came up to my house to play, which was understandable since I had neither toys nor a room of my own, but did have a little brother who always wanted to join in. I think my friends were also afraid of my mother. She spoke English with a heavy accent and looked severe next to their own pretty mothers. And, as I said, she didn't smile very often. I punched Terri Stroll in the stomach once because she said my mother looked like a witch. She ran crying to report my behavior to her mother, who probably told her she deserved what she got, because Ida never scolded me for it and never reported the incident to my mother. After that, I stayed away from Terri for a while. But I didn't really mind that we always played at Terri's or Ruthie's or best of all, outside where I could roam at will. I was always eager to uncover new places where I might escape my mother, and the more difficult to access, the better.

It hadn't always been like that, I suppose. Up until my brother was born, my mother and I had spent all of our time together, mornings in the apartment and afternoons in one of the many parks close by, or shopping for food almost every day. However, after my brother arrived, when I was about four, I was left to play by myself or with my new friends, from whom I soon learned English. And, out of my mother's sight, I could do all the things not allowed while under her scrutiny.

Climbing—fences, trees, ladders, rooftops—this was my consuming passion. By the time I was six or seven, I would regularly scale the spiral fire escape at the back of one of the buildings, all the way up to the third story. From there, I would swing onto the nearby telephone pole that bristled with iron spikes set into the pole to make it easy for workmen to climb, but that started too high up for me to reach from the ground. With one arm around the pole, I would lean out to survey both lanes and the street, never calling out to my friends when they came into view, knowing that any mother who might accidentally spot me up that pole would quickly report such perilous activity.

I acknowledged no danger. After all, what could happen to me now that Hitler was dead? No one could find me in the places I would hide. No one could reach me when I climbed higher and higher. As I had once been convinced of my capacity to bring my mother happiness, I was now certain of my own invincibility. Like the time I climbed over the wrought-iron rail of our balcony, high above Middle Lane. I was learning to walk the balance beam in gym class, and wanted to practice because the teacher said I was a natural. I had decided that the outside lip of our balcony was the perfect place to practice this newfound talent. Wiping her hands on her apron, my mother came into the parlor from the kitchen, spotted me on the wrong side of the rail, arms out, a seven-year-old tightrope walker, way above an imaginary cheering crowd. When she shrieked, I was so startled I almost slipped. The only word that came through clearly was ". . . . Hitler." My mother waited until I sheepishly climbed safely back onto the right side of the balcony before cutting off my escape. It took days for the welts on my backside, left by the strap she kept in the broom closet, to entirely disappear, although by the next day those welts were the only memory left of the punishment.

My mother had no qualms about hitting me. It was always for my own good, she said. Years later, regaling friends with my stories of daring-do, some would tentatively suggest that I might have been an abused child, but I never thought so. For one thing, my mother never remained angry for very long. She would hit me and then the issue, whatever it was, was settled. We could be hugging and laughing minutes later, unless I decided to sulk over the unfairness of life—something I never managed to sustain for very long, remembering my mother's stories about the hardships she had survived and the sorrow she was still suffering. What right did I have to complain? Did I not have food in my stomach, a warm, dry bed and two parents who loved me? These words now slip out as easily as Jell-o from Mrs. Williamson's warmed mold. They wriggle onto the page as if my mother were standing behind me, ensuring that I have gotten it right. She always said I would remember her words and it often surprises me how almost every day I manage to quote something she said, some phrase like "I cried because I had no shoes, and then I saw a man who had no feet." Somehow, her words had been blazed into my brain like the star on the glass door in the vestibule that forever altered my perception of what lay ahead.

One of the most frequent arguments we had revolved around the wearing of dresses. I simply wouldn't, except to school and on Sundays, when we went visiting. My mother's ongoing dialogues with God—in a voice loud enough for me to hear—only reconfirmed what I already suspected. I was a constant source of disappointment to her. Yet something stubborn and blind within my tough little body refused to bend to her will. Perhaps she had hoped that I would grow into a dainty little girl who liked to wear big, white satin bows in her hair and to play girlish games. Instead she had to contend with scraped knees, bruised elbows, and a strong resistance to wearing the new dresses my father would make at her insistence. How could I explain, without giving myself away, that dresses made climbing trees too difficult? I would simply insist dresses were for girls, as if that were sufficient to explain my position. But my mother would just carry on, pretending I had not spoken at all. My wishes were irrelevant. So I learned to keep them to myself. "What did I know of the world," she would say, and she knew what I would become if she didn't hold a tight rein. I would become a *vilde chayeh*, a wild animal. She knew what was best. And I knew I was no match for her tenacity in a head-on struggle. After all, hadn't she survived Hitler? How could you argue with that?

Sometimes, without knowing how it happened, perhaps sitting in the kitchen while she prepared supper, my mother and I would share an intimacy that would lift me out of my child's body and put us on an equal footing. We would travel back through time to a place where my mother still had hopes for the future, where everything was still possible, a time when she was young. She might tell me a story about her childhood or sing to me in her high, sweet voice, some

Yiddish song full of longing or drama. I loved her singing, although like smiling, she never did it often enough. My favorites were *Toiben shtayn oifen mein fenster*, Doves are Standing on My Windowsill, and *Pappirozzen*, Cigarettes, which to this day, can still move me to tears. It is a ballad about a young child, begging each passerby to buy his cigarettes, *trichen frum der reigen, nicht fargossen,* dry from the rain, not damp. He needs the money to feed himself and his little sister. The song tells of how his parents die, leaving them orphaned and wandering in the streets. At the part where he describes his little sister dying in his arms, I would dissolve, crying at the unspeakable horror of being left all alone in the world, alone and begging for acknowledgment. *Kupice, koifche, koif de pappirozzen.* Please, please buy a cigarette. Wrapped in her own sorrow, my mother, tears threatening to overflow the rim of her lower lids, would look at me strangely. For a moment, a light would come into her pale hazel eyes, sweeping over me like the beam from a lighthouse, then, just as suddenly it would disappear, as if returning to search inward for some memory to match the face before her with those buried deep in some unforgiving grave.

That's how we lived, surrounded by ghosts. They sat at the table while we ate our Sunday meal. They lay beside us in the bed as we slept, dreaming of flying through the air. They stood next to me as I watched my mother make the blessing over the Shabbos candles and at Passover, they crowded around her as she worked in the kitchen, changing the dishes and pots, and packing away the *chometz*. In the world I inhabited with her, they filled the space between us, binding and separating us until we could not distinguish between the past and the present. And those times, when my mother would grow melancholy and silent, I could see the ghosts sitting with her in the chair, whispering softly about how lonely they were, how much they longed to kiss her again, if only they could, one more time. And I would fight my helplessness with escape up a tree or onto the edge of the roof where I would sit, looking down at a world that passed silently by.

One bitter winter's day, I returned from school to find my mother lying in my bed with the comforter pulled up to her chin. Her eyes, red from crying, were as dark and vacant as the large hollow in my favorite tree.

"Mameh, are you sick?" I asked, alarmed, rarely having seen her lying down in the middle of the day. She looked at me numbly, as if we were strangers sitting opposite one another on a streetcar. I stood rooted at the foot of the bed.

"Mameh, what's wrong?"

My voice sounded strange to my own ears as she remained silent, the corners of her mouth slack. The skin on her face was almost as white as the pillow against which her hair now lay, spiked like shards of splintered wood. Her lids flickered as she pulled her mouth together in an effort to release some word stuck in her throat, but it could only manage to produce a small "oooh," a sound like the wind makes when it gathers its force to tear at the trees in autumn. From the foot of the bed, I slowly edged towards her, cautious in the event that any sudden movement might make matters worse.

One thin arm crept from beneath the covers. Clutched in my mother's fist with its knuckles rough and red from housework, was a photo. The arm dropped despondently onto the comforter, exhausted from the effort of reaching out. She opened the fist and let the photo fall. I picked it up gingerly. In it, two women were standing next to each other, neatly dressed. The one on the left had frizzy hair and a large nose that dominated her face. The other was tall, radiantly beautiful, shapely. Her dark hair was swept off a face that featured large, wide-set eyes that looked like they might have been blue. She wore a well-fitted, tailored suit, and on her left arm, an armband with a Star of David.

"Who are they, Mameh . . . who are these people?"

"Shaindel," my mother whispered hoarsely, "the one on the right is my sister, Shaindel."

So this was Shaindel, the beauty of the family. "But where is she, Mameh?"

With this, my mother began to cry, great heaving sobs that pulled at her chest, a doll being lifted by some terrible, invisible hand. Like someone was tearing at her rib cage to get at her heart.

"The letter . . . I got a letter," she said, lifting it from beneath the covers where she had buried it like a deadly secret. "I got a letter and this photograph. I thought she was alive . . . that they had made a mistake when they told me she was dead. But she is dead. The other woman who's in the picture, she lived, and someone gave her my address. She said that she thought I would want this picture of my sister. My dead sister, all my poor dead sisters . . . I have nothing . . . I am alone, all alone without my sisters who loved me. I am all alone."

She pulled the crumpled letter against her face. From some dark cavern, my mother let loose all her ghosts at once and they flew screeching into the room, swooping and howling with grief. The walls grew liquid with the heat of their anguish and shimmered like tar under the scorching eye of an August sun. The ends of their garments rippled past my face, leaving me shivering. Still, I would not let them bully me. My hands reached out to touch this woman I could not recognize, to find my mother's face buried beneath the surface of the twisted flesh thrashing back and forth on the wet pillow. And I held her face in my two small palms until the sobs subsided.

A WHOLE HEART

BOUNCE. BOUNCE. *Thwap.*

Bounce. Bounce. *Thwap.*

The rubber ball ricochets off the asphalt, hits the wall of the apartment building and with a stinging *thwap*, returns to Leah's outstretched hand.

The lane is empty except for a few sparrows, twittering on a clothesline. It's July. The asphalt shimmers in the heat and there's a deafening buzz that know-it-all Miriam says is insects, but Leah is convinced that it's the sound of a zillion voices squeezed inside telephone wires.

Bounce. Bounce. *Thwap.*

Leah has been alone in the lane all morning. In a continuous movement, she raises her arm, swipes at the sweat on her brow, and throws the ball.

In her shorts, a nickel is agitating, waiting to be spent on a Popsicle that she'll have to share with her younger brother when he gets home from day camp at three. Leah has refused to go to camp.

"I'm not going back," she had told her mother. "I don't wanna play stupid girlie games all day."

She braced herself for the sharp words, but her mother didn't respond in her usual way, only shook her head and gave Leah a funny look. Since she started working at the factory, Leah's mother had been full of surprises. This summer, they hadn't fought as much. It doesn't feel right. Her mother used to say that you have to fight to survive.

Leah has been hurling the ball all morning, a little harder each time. The harder the throw, the more stinging the catch. Her palm glows red and tingles but she doesn't mind.

She rolls the rubber ball in her hand the way her mother rolls raw matzo balls. Leah misses her friends. Everyone's away in the country with their parents: Ruthie in Rawdon, Terri in Ste. Agathe, and the twins, Miriam and Myra, at sleep-away camp. Leah should be in Val David. That's where they always spend the summer. It's not fair. They should be in the country and her mother should be making matzo balls or hard-boiled eggs and dill pickle sandwiches for lunch while she and her brother swim in the river or comb the farmer's fields to catch and torment grasshoppers. On the weekends, Leah and her father should be digging for worms, fishing for perch. But this summer Leah is alone on the empty streets, all because her mother has to work. Nobody else's mother has to. Nobody else's mother makes breakfast and then leaves. She slips her hand into her pocket feeling for the safety pin and the apartment key. The hard, cool metal is reassuring.

On the street, a car rumbles by. Leah turns and runs down the laneway to spot it and catalog the color, a game she plays to amuse herself, but it's gone, so she races back to her starting point as fast as she can. Her heart pounds and she places her hand over it. Through the thin blouse, the thumping against her palm brings comfort. She thinks about her mother's sisters, dead in the war. Her mother talks about them all the time, about how much she misses them. Leah doesn't know how they died, wonders what it's like to be dead, not to feel anything, not anything at all. Forever. Her mother says to be dead is to be like a stone. Cold and unmoving.

Alone most of the day, Leah often races like a wild animal down the lane just so she can feel her heart, to be sure that she is not going to die.

Another car passes, but Leah ignores it and resumes throwing the ball.

Ruthie's family has a car, an old one with a running board. And they have the budgie, Tweetie. Ruthie, an only child, has a lot of everything. Even more than Terri whose parents own a country house. All Leah has is a younger brother and parents with funny accents who work all the time.

Leah's mother says soon they'll have something.

"A car?" Leah asks, hopefully.

"We need to make a living to make a life. First, we're buying a *business*," her mother says, losing patience. "That's why I have to work."

Leah thinks what her mother is saying is that when they buy the tailor shop, they'll have a "busy-ness." She tells her mother she doesn't want a busy-ness, that her mother is busy enough. She just wants to be in the country.

"Wanna play?"

Leah's head swivels around.

A scrawny boy is standing beside her in the lane. She didn't hear him coming.

"Maybe," Leah says warily.

She looks him over. She doesn't like sneaks and she's never seen this boy in the neighborhood before. She knows all the boys because they play baseball and tag with her in the laneways and alleys. He's shorter than her, and is standing with his hands behind his back like the old men in the park. He has a scrawny neck that's poking out of a worn, striped T-shirt and his head wobbles a bit like it was looking for a way to get loose.

"You just move here?" she asks. She's juggling the ball

like a hot potato. He watches her and she knows he wants to get his hands on it.

"No," he says.

"Where do you live?"

"Over there." He points to a street at the other end of the lane.

"Joyce Street?"

"No, the one after. Bernard." He kicks a stone with the toe of a scruffy brown oxford.

"Oh yeah? How come I never seen you before?" She puts the ball in her back pocket for safekeeping. The boy still has his hands behind his back and he's not looking at her.

"I dunno. We've lived here awhile."

"Oh yeah? Where do you go to school?"

He thinks for a moment. "Where do *you* go to school?" he counters defiant.

"I asked you first."

He grimaces. Trapped. There are strict rules to this game.

"I go to Edward VII. I'm going into Grade Four," and he peers at her demanding his fair share. "You?"

"I'm going into Grade Three," she says making herself taller, "at Guy Drummond."

After that, neither of them knows what to say so Leah takes the ball out of her pocket and they play Stand-O.

His name is Hermie and although they play for an hour, he doesn't win a game. He's slow and has butterfingers, can't hold onto the ball. And he runs zigzaggy like a girl. But he doesn't give up or get mad. Not like other boys do when Leah bests them. Sometimes they say they don't want to play anymore. But not Hermie. He stays until he gets too winded.

"I better get home."

Leah says, "OK. You better. I don't want you dying on me."

"Will you be here tomorrow?" asks Hermie.

"Yeah. Maybe."

After that, Hermie shows up every day except on weekends when he and his parents go to the country, ". . . for the fresh air," he says.

Leah stops running up and down the laneway. Anyway, Hermie can't run. She taunts him about it, says it's like playing with a girl. He says nothing, just looks at her, his head wobbling a bit. He never fights back and Leah starts to feel bad for being so mean, so every once in awhile she lets him win at Stand-O. When Hermie doesn't feel like running, they spend their time looking for insects and wounded birds to rescue.

One day, a coal truck stops alongside Leah's building and they watch as a load rumbles down the chute. When the driver turns away, Leah snatches a lump off the top.

"To draw with," she tells Hermie when he gives her a quizzical look.

They take turns with the lump, sketching on the pavement. Hermie draws a big face with lines for the body and limbs. Leah says it looks just like him, all skinny and funny, but he still doesn't get mad. Instead he gives her a lopsided smile. She sketches some birds and a big heart. Hermie looks at it a little sadly, takes the coal from Leah and adds a circle inside the heart.

"What you do that for? That doesn't belong there."

Hermie looks at what he's done, then turns away with a little shrug.

"You're a real goof."

Hermie shoots her an anxious look and Leah feels bad. She gives him a little shove with her shoulder.

". . . but you're a good goof."

His face brightens and she shows him how to wipe his hands clean on the grass of the front lawn.

One morning, while playing Stand-O, Hermie twists his ankle badly. He doesn't cry, but Leah can see it really hurts.

"Go ahead and cry," she tells him, "it's okay."

Hermie says it's not so bad, but he can't put his foot down so Leah pulls his skinny arm over her shoulder and walks him to his apartment building two blocks away.

The next day, Hermie doesn't show up, not the day after that either. On the third day, Leah goes to his apartment building, but she doesn't know his last name or which apartment he lives in, so she sits on the stoop and waits for someone to come out.

She's chewing on the inside of her cheek when the door opens and she feels a thump on her back. An old lady holding a poodle almost trips over her. The dog starts barking. Leah jumps up and rubs the spot where the door hit her.

"Steps are not for sitting on, young lady," the old woman says, not unkindly.

"I'm sorry," says Leah, "I'm waiting for my friend, Hermie."

Leah is surprised to hear herself call Hermie a friend. He's always been just Hermie.

"Hermie?" the woman says, "Oh, you mean Herman Schnitzer. Poor thing, they took him to the hospital again. It seems he's in there more often than he's out."

"Did he break his ankle?" Leah asks, worried.

"His ankle? Oh, no dear," says the old woman "it's his heart again. Poor child, to struggle so since birth. Never able to run and play like a child ought to."

"His heart?"

"Yes, dear. It has a hole in it and they can't fix it . . ." She sees the look of apprehension on Leah's face and gently adds, "but he's a fighter, your friend, Hermie."

Without even a thank you, Leah flies off the steps. She races for the safety of the laneway and runs all the way home. She doesn't stop until she gets to her front stoop. Blood is pounding in her ears and her whole heart is bouncing hard against her rib cage. She presses down on it with the palm of her hand and, for the first time that summer, dissolves into tears.

MR. GREENE AND THE STUDEBAKER

"SWEETIE, HAVE YOU SEEN the new family in the building?"

"Muhn-uhn," Leah replied, her mouth bristling with plastic stick pins. It was Saturday morning in the Alper kitchen and Leah was carefully curling a strand of Joyce Alper's streaked blond hair around a fat brush roller. Mrs. Alper barely waited for the answer; just kept on chattering as usual. Leah wasn't listening anyway. She was tuned in to the radio and a story about the wealthy Cubans fleeing to Florida since Fidel Castro had ridden into Havana on New Year's Day. Leah dreamed of such places, places she'd visited in her books. Cuba. *The Old Man and the Sea*. She loved Ernest Hemingway. One day she would buy a copy for own library, the one she had started in a corner of the bedroom she shared with her younger brother, David.

"We honeymooned in Havana," Mrs. Alper said, as if reading Leah's mind. "The beaches were so white and beautiful. I guess it'll be ruined now."

As she secured another roller, Leah tried to imagine white sand, something she'd never seen. That was hard to do on a morning when the world outside her bedroom window looked like a crystal palace. After a night of freezing rain, everything on usually drab Goyer Street had been magically sealed under a thick coat of ice; everything was magnified—the toad-like rows of four-story apartment buildings; the skinny, young maples; the sidewalks. The ice storm had transformed Montréal into a scene from one of her father's Russian fairy tale.

"They're Hungarians, I think."

While Leah was daydreaming about beaches, Mrs. Alper had changed subjects. "Hungarians?" asked Leah wondering how Hungarians got to Cuba.

"Our new neighbors, silly. The ones I've been telling you about? Weren't you listening? I was saying that suddenly Hungarians are arriving in droves. The revolution, you know."

"How come they're all only coming now? We learned about it in school last year."

"Really? Smart girl. Well, I guess it's taken them this long to get here."

Leah smiled, pleased with the compliment.

Mrs. Alper could switch subjects faster than Leah's mother could switch moods, but at least she didn't get mad if Leah didn't grasp the gist right away.

"So, have you seen her?"

"The new neighbor?" Leah asked, still trying to find the thread of the conversation.

"Yes, dear. The new neighbor. She's very pretty, y'know, if you like that kind of big-eyed, washed-out blond look." Mrs. Alper's own blond hair and raspy voice tended more toward brass.

"Her little boy is sweet, though. He must be around Abbey's age. I guess you'll have a new babysitting client."

"Ummm," said Leah, slipping the last plastic pin into the roller.

"You won't desert us, will you? You know how much the kids love you."

"I'll always keep my Saturday nights for you and the Levines," promised Leah. Saturday nights, Leah would babysit for one or both of the families, earning twenty-five cents per hour or a special rate of forty cents for the two. When working both, she was required to roam between the apartments, and that presented the ideal opportunity to raid two refrigerators for food she would never find in her own home. Snacking on those forbidden foods was a guilty pleasure, a guilt that was doubled when Leah developed a predilection for bacon, which she ate raw, a necessary precaution against detection. Best of all, Leah was able to stay up late and watch old movies on TV. What she wasn't learning from books, Leah was learning from the movies.

Mrs. Alper smiled at her personal hairdresser and drew deeply on her duMaurier as Leah ran a palm over the rollers. Satisfied with their tautness, she covered her handiwork with the plastic hood of the portable hairdryer. That's forty-three, she thought. After each setting, Leah did the mental arithmetic: one head, one dollar earned. Forty-three dollars meant only another twenty-two heads to go before she could buy that Olivetti portable typewriter. A new family could help her get there sooner, she thought, maybe even by spring.

In the hallway, trapped indoors by the threat of iced-over, sagging electrical wires and sidewalks like skating rinks, the kids in the building played floor hockey. Their excited shouts bounced off the painted concrete walls that, here and there, revealed a few low gouges where sizzling pucks had left their mark. Leah called down over the railing to her brother.

"Not so loud, David, or the janitor will get mad." Her voice had a mother's authority. At one time or another, she had taken care of each one of the kids in the apartment building. In moments, their shouts escalated again, and Leah tried to remember when she last felt like playing. Her mother had repeated over and again that at twelve, she was already a grown-up and, therefore, had to be responsible, especially for her brother who, being four years younger, could not take care of himself. And if she wanted anything extra in life, her mother pointed out with annoying regularity, she would have to find a way to get it on her own. These days, all Leah wanted was a typewriter and a little time left to herself without having to "do something" for her mother.

Lettie Levine was patiently waiting, seated at her kitchen table with hair wet and a basket of rollers. The Saturday routine was as reliable as a Timex. Leah always did Joyce Alper first, put her under the dryer and then set Lettie ("Don't call me Mrs. Levine," Lettie had pleaded, "That's my mother-in-law.") By the time she was under the dryer, Mrs. Alper would be ready for her comb-out. Leah took pride in her skill with hair—especially the money she made—but she hated the comb-outs. Her own hair was so thick it tangled if you looked at it sideways her mother said, so she couldn't understand why anyone would deliberately want to knot up their hair, all that torturous teasing, the smoothing over of the topmost hairs, and then spraying it all into a solid helmet to make it last a week. And all the while, Lettie Levine would be giving her "helpful hints" on everything from how to practice good personal hygiene to the importance of making friends, all gleaned from *Good Housekeeping* magazines that she saved in a stack on a shelf in the kitchen.

"You don't mind some big sisterly advice," she'd say,

"because I truly believe that you spend way too much time alone." That was how Lettie usually started her lectures.

"I'm not alone," Leah would disagree, remembering to keep a smile pinned on her face. "I have lots of friends."

"Yeah," Lettie would say, "but they're all in books."

Leah met the new neighbor one blustery, cold day after school. The woman was struggling up the walk with a grocery bag under one arm and her young son, bundled against the cold in several layers of scarves, in the other. The wind was blowing hard but Mr. Gauthier, the janitor, hadn't got around to spreading salt on the walk yet. Sometimes it took him days to remember. Leah ran into the lobby and found the wooden doorstop. She wedged it hard into the crack under the door, then ran back and relieved the new tenant of her groceries. She was rewarded with a dazzling smile that left her breathless, gazing into the most gorgeous face she had ever seen. Although Leah had often been warned not to stare openly at people, she couldn't help it. The green eyes smiling at her tilted skyward above high, round cheekbones, rosy from the cold. A spill of blond hair dodged out from beneath a weary little blue beret framing a fine porcelain complexion. In the earlobes, angry red from the cold, Leah spied two perfect pearls, the same lustrous pinky-white as the small, even teeth of the woman's smile. *Photoplay Magazine* was the only place that Leah had ever seen anyone so beautiful.

"Thank you, thank you," the woman said with a Zsa Zsa Gabor accent. "What I would do if you not here, you sweet girl? My poor Tomasz is almost frozen—so cold, this Canada. I will never become used." She stood a moment in the foyer, catching her breath and juggling the baby from one arm to the other.

"I am Katya Horvath. What is your name?"

"Leah . . . Leah Smilovitz. We live in apartment 32."

"How lucky for me you here, Lila. Will you help me to take parcel up the stairs?"

"Sure."

Leah didn't correct the mispronunciation of her name; Lila sounded so . . . so exotic.

The three-room apartment on the second floor was in the back and looked out on a bleak collection of rectangles—the rear lane, a parking lot, and the back balconies of the buildings on Barclay Street. The apartment was a somber contrast to the sunny disposition radiating from Katya Horvath, and from what Leah could see, it was more sparsely furnished than even the Smilovitz's living room. The Horvaths had two mismatched upholstered chairs huddled together miserably in a corner. An old beige couch stood against the wall and had been draped with a large cloth heavily embroidered with colorful birds and red flowers. The throw was the only spot of color in the room, although it failed to hide a blossom of brown stains. Above the couch, a framed photograph, perhaps hung to fill the emptiness, somehow only managed to accent the bareness of the room. In it, a large family group was on an outing in the countryside, relaxing in preparation for a picnic that had been laid out at the photo's edge. People were sprawled lazily on the grass, unaware that a photographer was about to commit them to memory for a naked wall in Canada.

With a crooked finger, Katya beckoned Leah into the kitchen where she gently set down the grocery bag on the worn gray Formica of the table. Leah waited, although she had no reason to stay.

"Sit. Please. Do you want Coca-Cola, maybe? I have Coca-Cola." Katya's hand was already on the handle of the fridge.

"No, no, thank you," said Leah although she would have loved a forbidden Coke. Instead she pulled out a kitchen chair. There was a small rip on the vinyl, the tear held together by a strip of surgical tape. Leah sat on the edge of the chair and looked around the kitchen.

"How old you are, Lila?" Katya's eyes glowed dark green as they took in her young rescuer. It set Leah to fidgeting with her hair. She hated revealing her age and having to deal with the inevitable look of surprise that adults never felt the need to hide. She was invariably younger then they thought. Why did adults believe that telling a kid they looked older, as she so often was told, would be considered the ultimate compliment?

"Twelve," Leah said, almost swallowing the word.

"Twelve? That is such a special age when you are between young girl and woman, but already you are young woman . . . a beautiful young woman."

Leah looked up quickly to make sure she wasn't being mocked. The two studied each other openly for a moment until Leah lost her nerve and dropped her gaze.

"You are old enough to sit on my Tomasz. Yes? You sit on my baby?"

Leah giggled and then stopped herself, afraid she might appear to be rude. Her mother hated it when Leah laughed after she mangled a phrase.

"You mean *babysit for* Tomasz."

Katya smiled broadly and said, "Yes. I mean babysit. Maybe you can help me, sometimes babysit and help me also to practice with my English, no? You come visit me soon, yes?"

"So what's she like," Joyce Alper wanted to know, pulling on a freshly lit duMaurier.

"She's very nice," Leah said, slipping the tail of the comb into Mrs. Alper's hair, neatly slicing off a section and wrapping it tightly around a roller. Mrs. Alper tilted her head up at Leah.

"And?" she prodded.

Leah had never before minded gossiping a little with Mrs. Alper (usually about her friend, Lettie Levine), but now, for some reason, it felt wrong to talk about Katya. Her mother would say, "*Schvag* once in awhile. It makes it easier to listen and maybe you'll learn something." She was forever being reminded that no one needs to know your business. "Don't reveal so much about yourself, our family life, what goes on in our home. You're old enough to know better."

"Are you doing her hair?" Mrs. Alper asked. "She certainly needs to get rid of that *mochie* hairstyle now that she's in North America. Ow! Leah! Careful, that roller's way too tight."

"Sorry," said Leah, but there was no more talk of the new tenant.

Leah turned the unlocked doorknob to the Horvaths' apartment and walked in without knocking. She had stopped knocking a month ago.

"Lila?" Katya called from the kitchen. "Come see what Tomasz learned to do today. Look how clever he is . . . only ten months old and already standing like a soldier." She said this just as Tommy's stubby legs gave way beneath him. He looked up to see what he should do—laugh or cry. Katya's grin reassured him and he pulled himself up again, smiling with confidence.

Katya swept her son up in a big bear hug, then pulled Leah into the circle as well. The three of them twirled round and round. Thrilled, Tommy threw back his head and laughed and laughed until the women became infected with his joy and joined in. After a moment or two, Katya had to stop.

"Isn't he wonderful?" She kissed his strawberry blond curls.

Wonderful, of course, came out "vunderful," which always gave Leah a little thrill. She adored Katya's accent. It reminded her of old movies like *Casablanca* with Ingrid Bergman. That's how she described it to her friend Maxine Kastner at school during recess. Leah did a flawless imitation of Katya's accent that made Maxine giggle.

"If you like accents so much, how come you don't like your mother's accent too?" Maxine, whose parents had been born in Canada, could be really dense sometimes—and Leah told her so. There was nothing exotic about a Jewish-Polish accent, explained Leah.

"Well, you must really like her a lot, this Katya, because you never hang out with me after school anymore. Is she paying you to be a mother's helper?"

"Yes, I like her a lot and no, I don't take money from my friends. I help her because I want to, but even if that wasn't true, you know I would still have to take care of my little brother after school. Y'know I have to go home and hang around the apartment building. Just in case." Maxine made a face that said "poor you" and for once, Leah was relieved to have David as an excuse. Maxine was one of the few friends she had made since switching to Bedford School and she didn't want to lose her.

"Well, I think that's really mean of your mother to make you do that," said Maxine. Leah did not disagree.

When she thought about it, and she thought about it a lot, Leah couldn't remember how it was she ended up in Katya's apartment every day after school. But suddenly, coming home was something to look forward to. Before Katya, Leah had to be home straight after school to make sure David had his milk and cookies when the Hebrew Academy school bus dropped him off (because fattening him had become her responsibility too, when her mother started working five years ago) and she also had to do her homework. But all that resentment she felt over her list of responsibilities had magically evaporated. Because when everything was all done, she could run downstairs to Katya's, and while her friend prepared supper, Leah would help out by keeping Tommy entertained. Hours melted away as they talked about their favorite movies stars or shared plots of films they'd seen and books they had read. One day, Leah told Katya that she'd just finished a book called *Lady Chatterley's Lover*. There were some pages torn out here and there, but it didn't seem to matter to the story.

"I do not know that book," Katya said.

"I'll lend it to you." Leah was always excited to be able to share something with Katya, a new English word or a story she had never heard.

When Katya saw the cover of the pocketbook, a line

drawing of a man lying on top of a woman, she asked Leah, "Where you get this book?"

"I found it in a pile someone had left in a garbage can out back of the apartment," Leah said.

"Your mother, she know you read this?"

"Sure. It's okay. I know about sex. Lettie Levine explained it to me because there was an article in *Good Housekeeping* that said it is better to learn about the birds and the bees from someone you know. My mother didn't like the cover but I told her that our teacher, Miss Forbes, said never to judge a book by its cover and, besides, this book is a classic."

"A classic? Really? How you know?" Katya looked serious, but there was a smile playing in her green eyes.

Leah pointed to the quote on the top of the cover. Right under the words "Banned in Boston" was a line exclaiming: "A true classic!"

"Besides, I'm old enough to read any book." Leah didn't like to be reminded that there might be anything that could come between her and Katya, especially not her age. "But, I didn't really find it was that interesting. I guess whoever threw it away felt the same."

Katya laughed. It was a high, light sound that made Leah think of Tinkerbell and fairy dust. Along with the sliced apples Katya prepared for them, laughter was part of their daily menu usually preceded by Katya's mangling of an English phrase. "I have bells in my batter," she said one day after Tomasz had been cranky from teething. Leah doubled over and couldn't stop laughing. Katya joined in as she always did. She found the odd images English expressions conjured up endlessly fascinating, so Leah worked hard to find more of them to tickle her, phrases such as "cool as a cucumber," "bite the dust," and "in harm's way."

When Leah had first started school, her mother proposed that they practice English together. They would take turns testing each other on spelling and would laugh when one of them made a mistake. They had fun together, spending time pouring over Leah's homework. Back then, before her parents bought the tailor shop, Leah had a memory of doing everything together. Now "The Store" was like a living thing that needed constant care. Just a month after they bought it, her mother told Leah she was old enough to take care of herself and David. That way she and Tateh could take care of The Store and make a good living so they could have food on the table and a better life. When they moved, it was from the apartment located beside the tall trees of Lajoie to this one with the reed-thin saplings on Goyer Street. And at twelve, Leah still had to share a room with David, who was not only a boy, but also a little kid. But since Katya and she had become friends, Leah no longer minded The Store so much. If David hadn't needed to be fed and watched so he didn't wander too far away from the safety of the building, Leah would have spent all her after-school hours with her new friend.

"I am so happy not to be lonely with only Tommy. You

are so good for us," Katya said one day. Leah's heart felt like it might burst through her blouse. She understood what lonely felt like, especially because Katya's husband, Tibor, was always away, working long hours like her parents. But he was studying to be a doctor, Katya said, and never came home before ten at night and sometimes not at all. When he wasn't working at the hospital or in a clinic somewhere in the East End, he would be studying at the McGill Medical Library.

"He was half a doctor in Budapest, with only two years more to end," Katya told her one afternoon. Leah didn't correct her as she usually did—as Katya had insisted she should. This time, she sat quiet, listening.

"And then, the revolution. It change his life, change our life, change everything." Katya told Leah the stories as she peeled carrots for a thick, vegetable stew, a staple of almost every dinnertime. She chopped onions while she talked about her brother, too, and how his life had not been changed but ended. Her eyes welled up, but Leah couldn't be sure if it was from the memory or the onions; Katya didn't make any crying sounds, she just kept slicing.

"His life, it was squeezed out of him under a Russian tank, broken. Like all our hopes. He stand in harm's way. Is that right?" she asked, looking down at Leah. "He try to make change for good in the world, but why he not think more to change himself? What good does he make now he is dead and I am without brother, without father and mother? Even my Uncle Gabor, the one who sponsored us, he die one year after we come to Canada."

It was another war story. War stories were everyday territory for Leah. Her parents—her mother mostly—had been telling stories like these for as long as Leah could remember. Only the accent was different. And one more important thing. The Hungarians Katya described, her face pink with emotion, had fought back against the Russkies. Leah felt a small surge of pride when Katya said that many of the young men who fought and died were Jewish. So they were like the Israelis, Leah said. She did not say what else she was thinking, that they were not like the Jews of Poland and Lithuania, people like her relatives, who had died in the war without putting up a fight. How could that happen? Leah wondered about it over and over again. Why couldn't they—why didn't they—rush the guards? Why? She never asked the questions out loud because that would be disrespectful to the dead. But if she didn't ask, how could she ever understand?

More questions. And all of them made for a huge source of guilt, and the guilt itself was an endless well of frustration. Maybe these were the family secrets her mother did not want others to know about.

Katya's relation to the heroes of the Hungarian Revolution added a movie-like flourish to the story of her life, but the rest of it—the fleeing at night with her fiancé, the hiding in fields and slipping across the border into Austria— that all pretty much sounded like the stories told by Leah's mother. Except. Except Leah's mother lost her husband and then her son. For Katya it was the reverse; she had escaped, then married and given birth to a son in Canada. Despite all that hardship and abiding strength, there was something fragile about Katya that appealed to Leah. For one thing, she seemed to look to Leah for guidance. They were friends trying to help each other. There was no tug of war here like there was with her mother. And since he was never around, Leah didn't even mind sharing Katya with Tibor.

"We love each other since we are your age . . . ah, my sweet Lila, you know that is now half my life!" Katya said, her knife poised in midair above a bunch of carrots. Katya sometimes would go silent, eyes wide as if she had found something fascinating while walking along a path.

"And now we have Tomasz. What a blessing that we are alive. But to tell true, it is hard here. So hard to make a good life with no money, no family but we have good friends. Yes?" She beamed at Leah.

"We want so much to make for life better," Katya said with a little smile.

"A better life," Leah corrected automatically. This too sounded like her parents' story.

Miss Forbes, Leah's homeroom teacher, stood patiently at the front of the class, waiting for everyone to settle down. Her usually sober face, pockmarked with the scars of teenage acne, wore a smile that looked pasted on as she introduced a new student to the class. Anna, she said, had just arrived from Ireland, where she had been in a refugee camp for Hungarians waiting to come to Canada. Miss Forbes' chirpy introduction made the new student sound like a parcel delivered as a special gift to the class, but it was clear that the new girl would rather be anywhere else, maybe even back in Ireland. Leah's teacher placed two bony hands firmly on Anna's quivering shoulders as if thwarting any possibility of escape. Helpless, Anna's own hands hung loosely by her side, as stick-straight as her light brown hair, held in place with a small, white satin bow. Her mother probably thought putting the bow there would make her daughter more appealing, but the only effect it had was to set off a contagious ripple of giggles from some of the girls in the class, the same ones who always stuck together at recess and after school and played at one another's houses. They giggled knowing Annette Funicello wouldn't be caught dead with anything like that satin bow in her hair.

Two angry, red spots bloomed on Miss Forbes' cheeks. Staring at the offenders, she solemnly described to the class how Anna had walked across half a country at night, hiding in forests during the day. She had lost everything familiar in her life, Miss Forbes said, glowering at the tittering offenders. Could they imagine what that must feel like?

Leah felt sorry for Anna, but for the first time she understood what other kids had always known and taken for granted—how good it felt not to be the one who's different.

"*Voh hast du gevein?* You are never home any more when I call," her mother said. Leah's mother spoke Yiddish whenever she was on the attack. She spoke Yiddish more often than not. When she used English, it was for practice, all the better to be able to "handle" her customers. It was the only time Leah was ever allowed to correct her mother.

"*Ich bin immer du.* I'm always here. Where else can I be?" Leah answered in Yiddish, one of three languages spoken in the Smilovitz household, Yiddish being the language used the most. But Polish was the language of choice for her parents when they wanted to have a private conversation. Despite not knowing it, Leah somehow always seemed to understand what they were saying, maybe because she wasn't supposed to. She and her brother spoke only English and even though both his children were raised in Montréal, Tateh only spoke Yiddish "so you shouldn't forget where you came from." Leah, for her part, always answered in English so she didn't forget where she was.

Stepping into the bare vestibule of the Horvath apartment, Leah heard Katya call from the kitchen, "Who is there?"

"Me," Leah answered, feeling inexplicably annoyed. Who else could it be?

"Ah, here's my Lila." Katya was waving her into the living room. "Come, my friend, meet our wonderful Mr. Greene." Katya's cheeks were glowing pink as she pulled Leah by the arm and encircled her shoulders. "This is my dear, dear young friend who has been so much help for me. Lila, meet our dear friend, Mr. Greene."

Katya was squeezing Leah like an accordion, so Leah tried her best to smile her most sincere smile. After months of hearing his name mentioned, she was finally meeting Mr. Greene. Katya had been talking about him more and more lately, had even told Leah that Mr. Greene was becoming a very good friend to her and Tibor. He was an angel, she said, a kind and generous man who seemed to always be right there when they needed help. These words, vaguely familiar, created a little well of anxiety in Leah's heart. Perhaps it was because Katya's tone carried the same reverence that her mother's voice had whenever she talked about Henry Kalman, her father's landsman, Tateh's countryman, who had struck it rich "in America." It was he who had financed the purchase of the tailoring business, loaning her parents the money at a very favorable rate of interest.

At Katya's introduction, Mr. Greene pivoted on the stained sofa and threw a ready-made smile in Leah's direction. She smiled back but sensed that his eyes were looking right through her. The feeling was confirmed when, with a flick of his lids, he refocused his gaze on Katya. Leah flushed hotly at being dismissed like a child who had stumbled into a group of adults. She looked to see if Katya had noticed the slight, but her friend continued to chatter on, sometimes waving her arm in Leah's direction. Invisible, Leah took the opportunity to steal glances at the intruder.

MR. GREENE AND THE STUDEBAKER

Mr. Greene looked nothing like she had imagined. Katya's praise and his name, with such a kindly ring to it, had led Leah to imagine someone like her school principal, Mr. Graham, tall and handsome, or like Jim Anderson on the TV show *Father Knows Best*, all kindness and consideration. She had not expected to find this bull-like man in a shiny, striped suit creating a deep depression on the edge of the couch. He was leaning forward, his elbows on his knees and his hands clasped like they used to have to do in class for school prayer sessions. She had always felt like a real faker, pretending to pray, pretending to believe "Jesus loves me, this I know." Now she had to pretend she didn't mind Mr. Greene being there after school—during her time with Katya—didn't mind this man with the sparse, spiky gray hair bristling from the top of his large head. The hairstyle was called a crew cut. David had wanted one but Leah's mother said it would make him look like a Nazi. The top button of Mr. Greene's shirt was too tight. It looked ready to pop beneath a tightly knotted, skinny black tie. Leah thought it made Mr. Greene's too-large head look like it might explode out of his collar at any minute. What a square, Leah thought, and was forced to swallow a giggle. But it was true. There was a squareness to his body that could even be seen in the shape of his teeth, which he displayed prominently as he spoke. Leah was fascinated by them. They were large and ground down like the kind seen in the mouths of cartoon mules. She didn't like Mr. Greene at all, but there was something about his voice. It was a deep rumble and surprisingly soothing; it almost made her change her mind about him because it reminded her of her childhood. It sounded like her father's voice, the way it flowed in a singsong way when she was young and Tateh would sit on the edge of the bed, telling her and David bedtime stories in the dark.

Perched on the arm of one of the upholstered chairs, Katya sat across from Mr. Greene, leaning forward precariously. She was almost bent over double from the effort of concentrating so hard. To Leah, she looked like she was under some kind of spell, because her lips were moving ever so slightly, as if reciting a prayer. When Katya concentrated really hard, her lips would mouth words almost as if she could better decipher some deep mystery by repeating to herself what was being said. Unaware of Katya's efforts to understand him, Mr. Greene continued to rumble on like a train that was running behind schedule. Words were pouring out of him, none of them of any interest to Leah, so eventually she got down on the floor with Tommy, who was happily playing with a new Dinky toy.

"Lila, you take care of Tommy tomorrow, please?" asked Katya. "Mr. Greene is so good to take me to Jewish Immigrant Aid Service. He says there are many things they can do to help us."

"Sure," Leah said. "Any time. You know that."

"Good, then I'll pick you up at three-thirty tomorrow,"

said Mr. Greene, pushing on his knees and rising. Katya also stood up and stretched out her hand. Beside Mr. Greene, she looked like a birch against a boulder. When he took her hand, it disappeared inside his two square palms.

One night at supper, Leah's mother asked, "Is it true that you spend almost every afternoon in that Hungarian woman's apartment?" Lettie and Mrs. Alper had stopped her in the hall that morning as she was leaving for the store.

"Her name is Katya Horvath," said Leah.

"Hmm . . . Katya. That's not a Jewish name."

"Yes, yes, they're Jewish." Leah knew her mother's abiding distrust of anything, anyone non-Jewish.

"You can never tell with the Hungarians. So many *mischlings*, half-breeds . . ."

"She's definitely Jewish . . . and she's my friend . . . and no," Leah said, looking away, "I'm not there every afternoon. But I like being with Katya. She's like a big sister. We talk about things."

"What things?" her mother asked, switching to Yiddish, her eyes now drilling into Leah.

"Things. Like books and movies. We talk about her life in Budapest . . . Katya's very smart, y'know, she was going to be a biologist but the revolution . . ."

She stopped herself, seeing her mother peering down at her, drawing hard on her divining powers, searching for signs of danger. Leah kept silent, knowing that the more she said, the more ammunition her mother could store up for some future battle.

"Yes," her mother said. "Of course. Everybody was going be something great before they became a refugee. But if you want to accomplish something, nothing can stop you—not war, not empty pockets, not even the death of those you love . . . "

"Not even your children?" asked Leah, unable to keep quiet. Dismay filled her mother's eyes, and Leah realized that for the first time, she had won a point. She turned away from the victory, ashamed.

Leah started noticing small changes in the Horvath household. The embroidered cloth that had tried so hard to enliven the beige couch was now draped over a nearly new, red sofa and like magic one day, filmy white curtains appeared to blur the sharp edges of the view from the window. Leah was also prospering. More and more she was being recruited to babysit Tommy, for which Mr. Greene insisted on paying her the incredible sum of thirty-five cents an hour. He did so despite Leah's protests that she didn't want to take any money for helping Katya.

"Please take it," Katya pleaded. "It will make me feel good to know you are not losing time for nothing." Leah just nodded. What she couldn't say, especially now that Katya was so happy, was that she didn't feel right taking money from Mr. Greene. Why was he paying her to babysit anyway?

Tommy wasn't his child. But some part of her was thrilled despite herself; she was getting so close to buying the typewriter. Still she also felt inexplicably guilty, knowing she was not earning the money honestly, because she didn't like Mr. Greene or his stupid Studebaker with its chrome bumpers polished so brightly they could blind you.

Leah was pretty much a stranger to automobiles, having been inside only a few cars a couple of times—inside an egg truck when her mother had arranged a ride to the Laurentians for the four of them with Hymie, the Egg Man. That was before they had The Store, when her parents rented a country cottage each summer and shared the expense with the Poznan family. Her parents didn't own a car. There was no need, as they could walk the five blocks to work. Being that close to the shop was why they had all moved to Goyer she was told when she complained about being uprooted. If they had to go somewhere, they all got on the bus that stopped at the corner of Goyer and Wilderton. That was how Leah would get to the library and the dentist. In the apartment building, only a few of the neighbors had a car. The Alpers had one that Mr. Alper needed for his work as a salesman, and Lettie Levine said that they were going to buy a second-hand car as soon as they bought the house they were saving for in a place called Chomedey. But on the whole, cars were a luxury and a mystery to Leah. Since Mr. Greene and his Studebaker showed up, they seemed more of a mystery than ever.

Once a week, Leah and Tommy stood on the sidewalk, watching as Mr. Greene threw open the door of the Studebaker for Katya to step inside, and when she did, it was as if Leah was witnessing her friend being swallowed whole. Leah and Tommy stood hand-in-hand on the sidewalk as the Studebaker drove off. Watching it disappear left a strange feeling in the pit of Leah's stomach. But she never asked where Katya was going. That way she wouldn't have to lie to Mrs. Alper when she started asking those sneaky little questions.

On Saturday mornings, Mrs. Alper would put Leah through the wringer. Who is that man who comes every week to the Hungarian's apartment? Is he a relative? Where is her husband? How come he's never home?

Leah tried to satisfy Mrs. Alper's curiosity without betraying her friend, but Mrs. Alper was hot on getting details.

"You're in that apartment more than you're home, Sweetie, don't you have eyes?"

"Not for things that aren't my business," Leah finally blurted out before she could stop herself. She was repeating one of her mother's expressions, but then felt guilty without knowing why.

"Well," Mrs. Alper said, sitting up straighter in the chair, "aren't we getting a little touchy! I'm not being nosy, just curious as to what sort of people are living in the same building as my children. Besides, what's to get upset about if there's nothing going on?"

It wasn't like Leah hadn't been invited into the Studebaker during those times when Mr. Greene would take both Katya and Tommy on outings.

"We're going for a ride up to the mountain," he would say in his rumbling train of a voice. Leah loved Mount Royal. When she was younger, on hot summer days, the family used to take the bus up to Beaver Lake and spend Sunday afternoons along with half the immigrants in Montréal. They would lie around on old, scratchy blankets eating hard-boiled eggs and pickle sandwiches. But going with Mr. Greene held no appeal. There was something that always stopped Leah from climbing in to the Studebaker. She used David as an excuse. It came in handy so she wouldn't have to lie, but the last time, it was something else. David was playing at a friend's house and Katya was being persistent, trying to coax Leah to join them.

"We'll go for an ice cream after," Katya said with a sly smile, knowing Leah's weakness.

A whisper of cool air escaped as she stood deliberating at the yawning entrance to the car. A part of her wanted to go, but her feet were stuck to the sidewalk like melted gum. The interior of the Studebaker reminded her of the open mouth of a shark. It was like some dark secret she didn't want to know.

"I have too much homework," she said, "another time maybe."

Coming home from school, Leah's heart would sink a little if she caught sight of the black Studebaker. Sometimes it would arrive just as Leah was at the door and she would help Katya carry bags of groceries, and sometimes toys for Tommy, bought on St. Lawrence Boulevard. But most of Katya's afternoons with Mr. Greene were spent on some immigration matter resulting from the death of their sponsor, Uncle Gabor.

"That's why Tibor worry so much about having not enough money," Katya confided. "Since my uncle die, my cousins want nothing to do with us. They afraid we want money."

Leah's afternoons were slowly slipping back to where they had been before Katya and Tommy had filled them with giggles and stories and wordplay. They were "all gone," like Tommy would say after finishing a meal. It felt like her life had been whisked away by Mr. Greene and his black Studebaker. Unless she was asked to babysit, Leah stayed away from the Horvath apartment. That started on the afternoon she had turned the handle of the front door and found it locked. She had looked up at the number on the door, thinking she must be on the wrong floor. Where could Katya be? The Studebaker was parked outside. She had thought about knocking, but something made her decide against it. She didn't want to risk the possibility that no one would answer.

"Tateh, will you teach me some Russian words?" Leah asked. It was Sunday morning and her father was seated in the living room reading the *Kanader Adler*, the Yiddish daily. It was one of his greatest moments of pleasure in the week, especially if he could share a story or a poem with Leah.

"*Tochterel*, suddenly you're interested in learning *Russische*? *Voss epes*?"

Her father had tried several times to teach his daughter Russian but they never could get past *da*, *nyet*, and *spassiba* before Leah would lose interest.

If it had been her mother asking how come she wanted to learn some Russian words, Leah would not have answered. But she could trust Tateh not to use the information given freely as a weapon at some other time.

"Oh, I just thought it would be fun to surprise my friend, Katya. She learned Russian in school, growing up in Budapest."

"*Azoy*? So what do you want to learn how to say?"

"Tell me how to say 'I love you.'"

Walking home from school, Leah watched her feet as she placed each step carefully over the cracks in the sidewalk. It was an old game: step on a crack, break your mother's back. She thought she heard her name called and looked up, surprised to see Katya coming toward her with Tommy toddling alongside, fast as his little legs could go. Katya's face was shiny with a fine film of perspiration. Unable to keep up, Tommy suddenly stopped and pulled on his mother's arm. Without looking down, Katya urged him to keep going. Then he saw Leah and smiled broadly showing all his new teeth. In his excitement, he started to pull Katya forward. Leah laughed at the sight of Tommy rushing to her. A feeling recently forgotten bubbled up and was reinforced when Katya reached out to hug her.

"I need help from you," she blurted out.

"What is it?" Leah said, suddenly serious. Katya needed help and Mr. Greene was nowhere in sight.

"Look," said Katya, thrusting out her free hand. The long, narrow fingers uncurled and Leah saw one perfect, pink pearl earring.

"I've lost it. Ohh, Lila, I look everywhere . . . everywhere. I must find it. This earrings my mother give me and I never take them off. Never. I cannot lose them. I cannot lose this too."

Katya's eyes were brimming and now that she was close, Leah could see the red, swollen lids. Her friend looked like a little girl. Leah reached out to hug her as Tommy stood by quietly watching, uncertain as to whether he should cry too.

"We'll find it," Leah said in her best motherly voice. "We'll look really hard and we'll find it."

But several hours later, after turning over sofa cushions, airing out bedding and moving furniture, no pearl earring was anywhere to be found.

"Maybe you can make a pendant out of the one that's left," was the best Leah could offer to console her friend.

A week later, Katya was all excited with some news she wanted to share. Since the earring incident, Leah had begun dropping by after school again. She didn't mind so much anymore that her friend was often preoccupied, not so predisposed to laughter or practicing English phrases. She was just happy to have time with Katya and Tommy. Katya's news was that Mr. Greene had found Tibor a new position in a clinic nearby, working for an old Hungarian doctor.

"Now Tibor will not spend so much time traveling on a bus," Katya said, chewing nervously on her lip, a newly acquired habit, "and so he can spend more time at home with our little family. I miss him so much, Lila. So much.

"It is not easy to be all alone, without family. I never see my cousins since their father die. I never get used to being without family. We don't want money from them like they think; we want our family. Maybe if we have money, they will not be 'fraid from us, and Tommy can grow up and know his cousins, his family."

Leah nodded, knew instinctively what Katya meant. Growing up without family meant you always had to hide your envy. Random comments like, "I have to go to my grandmother's house for Shabbat," or "we're going to visit my aunt this summer in New York" were like knives between the ribs. What hurt the most was how other people took the luxury of family for granted, or worse, resented the intrusion in their lives. Leah could not understand that at all. It was a case of somebody who was always hungry having to listen to the complaints of a person who had too much food to eat.

"Money, Tibor says, will make difference. When he become doctor, everything will be different. But it cost so much to live here. At least communism, they give free education. I want to help him but what can I do, Tommy is so young? I don't know anymore. Mr. Greene is so nice, he loan us a little money and bring toys for Tommy. He help us so much. I do not know how we can repay him."

When Leah collected the last dollar she needed to buy her typewriter, she run upstairs to share the good news with Katya. The door was open, a happy sign for Leah who found her friend in the kitchen, leaning against the worn counter, staring out the window onto the alley below.

"What's the matter?" The sight of Katya's stricken face made Leah forget all her good news. Katya just shook her head. A deep silence filled the space between them; it hung like the Tergal curtains in the living room, hiding something unpleasant. There was a disturbing familiarity in the way Katya looked. It was the expression Leah's mother wore before she got one of her nerve attacks, the kind that that made her mother do and say crazy things. It caused a strange detachment from the things and people around her. Seeing Katya that way scared Leah; she felt like she had swallowed something very cold too fast. Her stomach ached.

"Are you okay?" she asked again, refusing to be shut out, not by this woman, not again.

"What can I tell to you? You are only a child and it is not right for me to let you taste the bitterness in my heart."

"You can tell me anything," Leah said, "that's what friends are for. My mother says that it makes heartache easier to take when you share it with someone you love."

"Ah, my sweet Lila, how can I take away from you the last bit of your innocence? It is not right. I should not put you, how you say, in harm's way."

The tears that sprang to Leah's eyes surprised them both.

"Why won't you tell me what's wrong? What did I do? You are my best friend and I know . . . I know that's crazy because you're twenty-four and I'm only twelve, almost thirteen, but . . . "

Katya gathered Leah into her arms, hugged her close, and smoothed down the wild tangle of her hair.

"You are so, so young, but strong. Please understand . . . this is not to do with you, my Lila. How can you think you lose me as friend? Don't cry. Sit down here at the table.

Wipe your face. I will tell you something but this must not be told to anyone, not your mother, not to anyone, you understand?"

Leah nodded and wiped at her eyes with the back of her hand. She knew how to keep secrets.

"Tibor is in trouble. He do something that is not right and if anyone knows this, we will not be allowed to stay in Canada. Maybe they even put Tibor in jail."

Katya inhaled slowly, and stared at the worn kitchen table. She avoided looking at Leah as if she had been the one who had done something wrong.

"Tibor, begin to take care of ladies who are pregnant but do not want baby. Do you understand what I mean?"

"You're talking about abortions? I know what abortions are. My mother told me."

"Yes, abortion, and Mr. Greene say it is very serious if immigration know this . . . or the police. He say he must pay people to keep quiet. Tibor is very good doctor; no one is hurt but still, people talk and that is dangerous. So we must be careful and poor Tibor now must work more even than before." As she spoke, Katya turned her gaze to the window and the bleak landscape of rectangles beyond. "I don't know how we give back all the money Mr. Greene have to spend. We want so much to make a new life, better life . . . now I don't know. We make it more worse."

Leah said nothing. Not that day or after. She swallowed Katya's secret like the food she had to eat to be polite. She swallowed it without tasting it, but it never was digested properly. After that day, Katya slowly, silently slipped away.

In July, Katya told Leah that they were moving and because she asked with a gentle insistence, Leah finally agreed to take a ride in the Studebaker. She climbed onto the cool leather of the back seat, stretched so tight she slipped in without effort. Tommy was happily seated in the front between Mr. Greene and Katya. Mr. Greene's arm was casually draped over the length of the seat and almost imperceptibly, his hand lay on the back of Katya's neck. The gesture was so intimate, the color rose in Leah's face. She had seen this in the movies, but never in real life. It was the gesture of a man who knows what he owns. With his left hand, Mr. Greene steered the car into traffic. Leah sat mesmerised by the way Mr. Greene's arms could act so independently of each other, one controlling the steering wheel, one controlling Katya.

In the darkness, Leah braced herself on the expanse of cool leather. Her hands slid backward into the fold where the back met the seat, looking for something to grip, something to hold onto so that she could keep from thinking about what her eyes were seeing. Her fingers found something smooth and round. When she pulled it out, it shone lustrous pink in the cool darkness. For a moment, Leah fingered the smooth, perfect surface of the pearl then, silently slipped Katya's earring deep into the pocket of her shorts.

REMEMBER MY WORDS

THE JET ROARING over the Atlantic is filled with rambunctious university students and she can't stop smiling. All around, people are talking, laughing, and drinking the free liquor that started flowing as soon as the seat belt sign went off. It has taken a year of planning but she's done it, she's affected her escape from her mother.

Some guys stop by her row to talk to a friend.

"Where are you from?" they ask her.

"From Montréal," she says, surprised at their friendliness. "And you?"

They had all departed from Dorval airport, but she soon

learns that the student flight has drawn kids from all over the country.

Someone asks, "Are you staying in London or moving on?" and she can't help blurting out the answer, despite her mother's admonitions about giving away information that's nobody's business. "No," she says, "London is just a stopover to catch a flight to Tel Aviv."

"First time?" someone else asks and she wonders if it's that obvious, then, unable to contain her excitement, she tells them that this trip is her first "everything"—her first journey beyond Plattsburgh, New York, her first air flight, and the first time on her own.

"Cool," says one of the guys, "but don't go telling everyone that. This may be 1966, but a girl traveling alone should always be a little careful."

"Think more, talk less," her mother had said.

The stewardess offers her a choice of alcoholic beverages and she orders the only thing she knows, a screwdriver. She sips it slowly, savoring the sensation of being an adult. This moment is worth all the sacrifices she's made in the past year, working at the bank all day and babysitting on the nights she didn't have courses at the university. Her friends all said she was nuts going off by herself to Israel but she said, "What could happen between Montréal and Tel Aviv? There's only a small stopover in London. It's no big deal."

They land at six a.m., and some guys invite her to share a cab to the Students' Union. To her delight, the streets of London are unbelievably familiar to her from all the old British films she has watched growing up. For the sake of appearance, she tries to act the seasoned traveler with her cab mates but the sun rising over the rooftops, the pigeons flying over Trafalgar Square, do her in. She thrusts her head out the cab window and gawks in awe at Nelson's Column and the Admiralty Arch.

"There's Canada House," someone says. "That should be your first stop in London."

"But I won't need to do that." There's genuine regret in her voice. "I'm leaving for Israel this afternoon."

Less than an hour later, however, she is cramped up with fear, her regret forgotten. Sitting on her suitcase, she is weeping loudly because her Students' Union flight to Israel has inexplicably been postponed for a week.

She can almost hear her mother's derisive take on the situation. *"In life nothing goes as planned so, listen to me, hope for the best but expect the worst."*

"Listen," said one of the boys from the cab. She raises her red-rimmed eyes. The sight of his close-cropped hair, seersucker jacket, and button-down shirt somehow assures her he has good intentions. "Some of us are going over to a boarding house I stayed in last year. The rooms are clean and cheap at Singh's. And it's on Grosvenor Square, fairly central. Do you want to see if you can rent one until you sort out your travel arrangements?"

Not trusting herself to speak, she gratefully nods yes.

"You are traveling alone?" Mr. Singh asks when they reach the house and she inquires about the cost of a single room by the day and for the week.

"Yes, but I have friends studying here in London," she says. She knows no one in London and the guys from the flight are all off to different destinations over the next few days, but somehow having imaginary friends makes her feel safer.

Mr. Singh smiles broadly, revealing large white teeth the size of Chiclets.

"Is this your first visit?"

"Yes, but I won't be staying long." Something about the way he looks at her makes her want to deceive him.

"Well, if there is anything I can do to make your stay in London more pleasant, please don't hesitate to let me know. It will be my pleasure."

The next morning at breakfast, while getting suggestions on places to see and where to eat cheap, she becomes aware of a tall and sinewy young man, with curly black hair, moving in and out of the kitchen. Like a dancer, he travels around the small breakfast room, barely making a sound as he deposits dishes on the long table. Eventually, he places a breakfast of burnt toast and eggs swimming in oil in front of her. Mr. Singh watches from the doorway and she can feel his eyes on her. She tries to ignore him the way she ignores truck drivers back home who whistle at her and call out, "Hey, Baby!"

When the server returns to the kitchen, a girl from Chicago checks her out and giggles, "I guess you've noticed Michel. Isn't he gorgeous? An art student from North Africa. He works here for his bed and board. Too bad I'm leaving today 'cause he could work my bed and board anytime."

She's never heard anyone talk like that. She smiles but looks away, her heart racing.

Late in the afternoon, overwhelmed by the size and bustle of London, she returns after visiting Canada House and doing some sightseeing only to discover that she is one of only two boarders left. Everyone else has moved on. Mr. Singh suggests she have tea in the common room. "After all, it's included in the price of the room," he says.

As he pours the tea, he tries to make conversation but she is preoccupied, thinking about the information she has picked up at Canada House concerning the Student Union flights. They're erratic, she was told, and so she should keep checking in to make certain she doesn't miss the next flight to Israel.

"What did you see today?" Mr. Singh seems determined to intrude.

"The National Gallery," she says not wanting to be considered a rude North American, but she soon regrets having accepted tea, even if it was included.

"Ah! My favorite," says Mr. Singh, clapping his chubby hands. "Did you see Bronzini's sensual Venus and Cupid? You know, it is full of messages of love."

"I think I saw it," she says. "I saw so much. I don't remember."

"But that is such an important piece; maybe my very favorite." He starts analyzing the painting, prattling on about love and, in the slyest way, she thinks he is suggesting that he is a master in the art of lovemaking. But she's not sure.

"Love is most exciting at a tender age like yours. How old are you, dear?"

"Nineteen." She tries to make it sound like merely a number. His eyes fix on her full figure and mature features.

"You look older, m'dear, yes, you do."

Not knowing whether this needs a response, she shrugs.

Later that night, over a supper of bangers and mash served by the silent Michel, Mr. Singh seats himself opposite her in the empty dining room and returns to the subject of love and how patience and tenderness, as expressed in the painting—and as delivered by someone with experience, is a wonderful thing. She convinces herself that he is harmless because to take all this seriously would send her into Panicville, so she tries to imagine his stumpy body in scratchy red flannel underwear. It works, but her dinner, already unappetizing, becomes totally inedible. Mr. Singh tut-tuts over the food she leaves on her plate. Michel, silent as a zephyr, clears the dishes. His arm brushes her shoulder and she leans closer to hear him murmur an apology.

Her second day on her own, she is relieved when a new batch of boarders arrive, some of them from Canada. She overhears them arrange to visit a few of the sights. They tick them off from lists they made back home: The Mall and Buckingham Palace, The Tower, London Bridge, the Victoria and Albert. She asks if she can tag along and although the day is bright and she is elated at having companions, she is unable to forget for a moment that she is stranded.

Three days away from home and she begins to believe that nothing is ever going to go right again. She misses her friends, the taste of something familiar, money she doesn't have to count out three times. She misses feeling safe.

"Don't trust anybody," her mother said, her parting shot at the airport. "Especially when you are all alone. There is danger everywhere."

That night, Michel knocks at the door to her room, asking in halting English if she needs fresh towels. He stands in the door staring and doesn't leave even though she says, "No, no towels, thanks." He walks through the door uninvited, but she doesn't stop him. He asks where she's from and they begin an exchange and while they're talking, they somehow slip seamlessly from standing to sitting, then lying on the bed. He kisses her, at first softly, without insistence, and any entreaties and rebuffs are swallowed. His mouth is softer, warmer, wetter than any other she can remember kissing. He stretches out against the length of her and moves slowly. The friction soaks their clothes with fluids and sweat. His long, sculpted face, those dark chocolate eyes like shadows in a Casbah doorway, his thick, black curls hanging over her; his lean body sliding up and down as the heat sears her skin; the taste of his tongue in her mouth after he licks her neck and cheeks. Michel's slender, baby-soft fingers rub her neck and beat a soft tattoo on her shoulders until she feels the blood pound its way to the surface of her skin. There is a throb between her legs.

She wants to succumb, to let go of her cumbersome virtue, that parting gift, wrapped by her mother's rough hand. And why not give in? This far from that piercing gaze, her mother would never know.

He slides his hand down her arms, and she stiffens, ashamed of the hairiness he'll find there. "Non, non," he croons and runs his lips down the inside of her forearm, then hoarsely whispers how much he loves every hair, as only a North African can.

"Men will say anything to get what they want. They will use you and then, forget your name in a minute. Any woman who believes a man's words in the heat of passion is an idiot."

She pulls Michel roughly toward her, wanting urgently to believe in the moment, in the honesty of his mouth so tender one minute, so ravenous the next. She feels herself drift away from her past.

A creaking floorboard outside the door brings her roughly back to the reality of the room in Mr. Singh's boarding house on Grosvenor Square and to her vulnerability, lying beneath Michel. Her eyes fly open, but Michel's passion renders him deaf to any danger. She turns to the sound and strains desperately to see through the gloom. From beneath the door, she thinks she detects the shadow of Mr. Singh's squat body creep across the floorboards. Is he waiting his turn? Maybe he and Michel have planned this together. Would Michel have her and then pass her over to his boss? Terror succeeds in dousing her passion.

"Don't forget who you are. Don't lose yourself. Use your head."

Michel tightens his grip on her thighs and bows his head low to suckle a breast through the thin, damp t-shirt but suddenly, she sits bolt upright. Prompted by the imagined shadow of Mr. Singh, she announces they must not go on. From some old novel, she draws on a bizarre defense.

"I am impure," she blurts out. His eyes search her face for meaning. "I am bleeding," she lies. "My period, you know, period?"

Michel stiffens and pulls away, his eyes still wild and unfocused. He murmurs something, an apology maybe, as he quickly straightens up and tucks in his shirt. And then he is gone and nothing remains but the damp distillation of their juices on the sheets. She jumps up and locks the door, moving a chair beneath the handle as she has seen done in countless movies. She lies in bed and tries not to think of what her mother would say if she knew what had just transpired. And then she laughs, realizing that she has been guilty of conjuring her mother at those times she would never know about in reality.

"It's your mazel that I will be with you wherever you go, because you'll remember my words."

The next morning, Michel fails to show up for work and she decides it's her last morning in London. She has got to leave if she's ever going to get a decent night's sleep. Mr. Singh, receiving the news of her departure, redoubles his efforts to slip her fawning looks as she tries to force down another inedible breakfast of burnt toast and black tea. Mr. Singh's dark eyes glitter from deep within the folds of his cheeks and he bends close to refill her tea cup after every other sip, then draws back like a cobra, leaving behind a confusing whiff of cheap cologne and curry powder.

Chewing on a piece of toast, she wonders what has become of the silent Michel. She longs to see him again, to explain why she could not give in to his desire or her own.

"Such a marvelously historic city," she hears Mr. Singh say. She has learned to filter out most of his innuendos. "It deserves more careful scrutiny than you Americans have time for."

"I'm Canadian . . ."

"Yes, well the point is the same. How can you possibly have explored all of London in less than a week?"

"But I have my tickets," she lies. Since first arriving she has become good at fabricating misleading information. "I'm leaving for Greece."

She is not going to Greece and does not as yet have her tickets, but this morning, she's going right down to the National Union of Students' offices and onto any plane that will deliver her to her relatives in Tel Aviv.

"We have nothing going to Israel," says the pimply clerk at the NUS office, but one look at her stricken face and he adds, "unless you're prepared to go via Basel and Cyprus. It's a six hour layover in Nicosia."

"I'll take it," she says leaping at the chance to leave London and Mr. Singh behind, wringing his sausage fingers.

"You leave at four a.m. from Gatwick," he says as if it's perfectly normal for students to live like bats.

"What's another sleepless night?" she mutters under her breath.

In the gloom of the Air Basel cabin, someone squeezes into the seat next to her with a soft "Hi." She senses a male's long body making an effort to settle into the cramped space, but she doesn't turn her head. "Hi," she responds reluctantly and leans back against the darkened window. Her head is filling with thoughts of Michel. Regret is eroding her fear, which has conveniently evaporated now that she is safely out of Mr. Singh's reach.

The plane pulls itself off the ground with some effort, shimmying and shaking like the wings are ready to fall off. There is only one stewardess. In sharp contrast to the trim, young Trans-Canada Airlines hostesses, this one is middle-aged and chunky. The propellers make a shocking racket. They roar and rattle on the wing and appear unnecessarily wobbly as they spin. Outside the window, the blur of the blades and the lights of London winking a merry goodbye bring no comfort.

"Where are you from?"

The voice is deep and comes to her through the rumble as if from a great distance. She turns her head a little to confirm she hasn't imagined the question. In the dim yellow light she sees a camel tweed jacket, crisp, button-down shirt, burgundy knit tie, and above it, a good-looking, clean-shaven face. An Ivy League poster boy, she decides, and replies with the greatest of economy.

"Montréal."

And then, unable to stop herself from being polite, so bloody Canadian, she dutifully asks, "And you?"

"Philadelphia," he says, then adds enthusiastically, "Wow . . . Montréal.'

She feels him shift his body toward her.

"How about those Canadiens . . . What a great hockey team. And next year, aren't you guys hosting another World Exposition like the one in New York? Whaddya call it?"

She straightens her body and stares at the back of the seat in front of her. "Yeah, we're all excited about Expo '67," she concedes.

"So are you on your way to Israel, too?" he asks.

"Wherever you go in the world, if you find another Jew, you'll be safe."

The question throws her. How easily he asks without fear of exposure or offense. It is one of those things that she is learning distinguishes Americans from Canadians.

And then she wonders, do I look *that* Jewish?

"Yes, Israel," she answers as the lights go off in the cabin, and she closes her eyes to end any further conversation. Back home, she would have smiled coyly at someone so obviously desirable, telling him all about herself, where she came from, where she's going. Back home, she would be working to make him love her, want her. But she's far from home.

"What is happening?" she wonders, as she drifts into sleep and a dream. She is sitting on a porch swing, dressed in organza with a large satin bow in her hair, eyeing a detachment of soldiers walking past. One makes a quick half-turn and marches smartly toward her like a wooden soldier gone awry. He bows deferentially and seats himself beside her on the swing. In one smooth movement, his head is on her shoulder, nestling in close. His chin stubble scrapes against the satin of her bow but she enjoys the intimacy until she hears the snoring.

Snoring? Omigod! She wakes with a start, thinking, "I'm snoring!" Yet her eyes are open and she can still hear the soft, snuffling sound. Relief floods through her until she senses lips close to her ear and the brush of hair against her jaw. It raises goose flesh down her side. Suddenly alert, she feels herself once again under siege. There's a head on her shoulder and a marked pressure against her right thigh. She looks down. A large hand is lying palm up against her leg, the fingers curl inward like a child's. She doesn't want to wake him, doesn't want to hear the apology. Slowly, she shifts her shoulder nudging the head in some hope the body will adjust itself. Instead, the head nestles in closer to her chin until she can smell the scent of clean hair. She concentrates on the hand, on any possible movement that will recommend what she should do next. But the hand remains open, as if waiting for comfort. The clatter of the engines overrides her confusion and slowly, lulls her back to sleep.

The next time she awakes, she feels warmth not only on her neck, but also in the palm of her left hand. There is a soft pressure there that takes her a moment to identify. Fingers are loosely laced through hers. There is a feeling of well-being that belies her confusion. There is something familiar in the moment. She remembers walking into

Kindergarten class holding the hand of Larry Lipowitz, her first heartthrob.

Beyond the clanking propeller, a thin, orange line is separating the sky from the carpet of clouds below. They are heading into the sunrise. Soon, everyone will be awake. Something must be done, she knows, to break this intimacy with the stranger in the seat next to hers. This is a potentially embarrassing situation. But she cannot recall any words of wisdom on the subject. Her mother's voice is oddly silent. The only action she manages is to turn her head toward her fellow traveler. She is only a little surprised that his eyes are open and looking back at her.

HEBREW LESSONS

"WHY ARE YOU TWO SO SAD, Mameh? Mankeh?" Tamar asks, but our mothers are not listening.

Tamar refuses to be ignored tonight, the night before her wedding.

"Marriage? Isn't this what you groomed us for from the moment we were born?" Tamar tries again. But our mothers are still not listening. They sit with their elbows on the table, chins in their palms, telling stories about when we were babies. They're pulling out stories like sheets that have been sitting too long in the wicker chest we brought from Germany. One story after another is being unfolded, aired out, neatly replaced.

A little tipsy from a half-finished bottle of Mateus, Tamar and I are trying hard not to giggle at all the melodramatic weeping, but the more we try, the louder our mothers wail. Tomorrow Tamar weds Leon and leaves her family in Israel to make a new home here in Canada, in Toronto. My cousin Pola, Tamar's mother, is inconsolable, and my mother is aiding and abetting.

"Enough tears, Ima!" Tamar's shrill voice is up in the higher registers. "Stop. We'll soon need a mop."

But Pola can't stop. The first time we met, she was also in tears. It was in Tel Aviv's Lod Airport. Pola hadn't seen me since I was eighteen months and there I was, eighteen years old already. That was the summer of 1966, six years ago when Tamar and I first became friends. Unlike her mother, Tamar never cries but always has a suppressed giggle waiting to erupt. She lives in a state of perpetual grace, brightened by the anticipation of some golden future just around the next corner. From our very first encounter, she impressed me as someone skipping blithely through life, always trailed closely behind by her mother, whose task it is to right whatever has been knocked over or to sweep up the debris resulting from her daughter's unbridled exuberance.

This trip to Montréal is Pola's second attempt to marry off her daughter. Only last year, Tamar was engaged to a sullen native of Haifa who was living in Montréal. My father, at the urging of his sister Tzippah, Tamar's grandmother, had met with the prospective groom. It was not a happy meeting. Mild-mannered and affable, my father took an instant dislike to Tamar's fiancé and made dire predictions about the suitability of the young man with white flecks on the cornea of his left eye. But the warnings went unheeded until the groom bolted a week before the wedding. Despondent, Pola had revealed that the fiancé had suddenly demanded a large dowry.

When I heard the story, I grew furious on Tamar's behalf. My mother, however, had received the news in her usual stoic manner. She jutted out her jaw, drew her lips together tightly and rolled her eyes heavenward, as if to imply there was nothing to be done by us mere mortals. Her advice to Pola was to return the wedding dress immediately for a refund.

Seemingly unfazed by the cancellation of her impending marriage, Tamar had merely shrugged her shoulders and might have said something but for a fierce look from her mother. The wedding dress had been returned with some small loss on the deposit and instead of a groom, Tamar took home an expensive new Courrèges outfit. I had watched them disappear, Tamar doing a little hop as she waved goodbye. I imagined myself at nineteen, passing through those same gates, leaving with a spring in my step. However, my mother had not been ahead but behind me, held back—though barely—by a gate, shouting out her final instructions on what I was to do in order to return home safely.

Less than a year after her first matrimonial foray, Tamar has returned with a new Canadian groom, Leon, introduced to her in a Jaffa discotheque by somebody's cousin. The details of Tamar's newfound *mazel* were relayed one night while Danny and I were over at my parents' for Shabbos dinner. My father was translating a letter from his sister Tzippah, as my mother fussed over Danny, accusing me of not feeding him properly.

"Mankeh, please let me finish reading," my father said.

My mother shot him a look and then heaped more mashed potatoes on Danny's plate. Danny rolled his eyes, but dug in. My father continued his reading, a glowing description of the new fiancé as an up-and-coming businessman. My Aunt Tzippah was convinced that this time her granddaughter had met a suitable boy. But an involuntary arch to my mother's eyebrow, like a semaphore message, was transmitting disbelief. It silently questioned the coincidental meeting. My mother has that kind of power, the knack of negating your credibility with the mere twitch of a facial muscle. But I hardly noticed the exchange. I was wondering if the discotheque was the same club where I had met Moshe.

Tonight, we are sitting in my mother's kitchen. She and Pola speak in Yiddish, liberally sprinkled with their native Polish, as if their language alone can conjure up the narrow streets of the Displaced Person's Camp in Pocking. I was born there and Yosel too, Tamar's older brother. Tamar is a genuine *sabra*, however, conceived and issued forth on the holy soil of Israel. I think it gives her the luxury of a minor disdain for the past.

"*Iz dis de liddle girl I carried?*" Tamar sings, exaggerating the phrasing and stretching out her arms, pretending to stagger beneath the weight of an oversized baby. Tamar has had enough of all the weepy stories and breaks into song, belting out an off-key rendition of "Sunrise, Sunset." The song has recently become a staple at Jewish weddings replacing "Here Comes the Bride."

"*Iz dis der liddle boy at play?*" I scramble to join in, making a babushka with a dishtowel like in *Fiddler on the Roof*. But I can only manage to hang on to the line of harmony for a moment or two before doubling over with laughter. My mother peers over at us, but she too can't resist. She turns away from the weeping Pola and begins to hum along, chuckling under her breath and wiping away tears caught in the creases of her eye.

"They're right," she finally says to Pola.

"Who is right?" asks Pola, her voice thick with sorrow.

"Our daughters. What's there to cry about? Your Tamar is getting married and soon you'll *shep naches*, handfuls of joy. You'll see, it'll all work out for the best."

"That's easy for you to say, Mankeh," Pola blurts out, noisily blowing her nose into a shredded Kleenex. "Leah still lives in the same city as you. And didn't you once tell me how before the war, when you wanted to make *aliyah* to Palestine, you didn't leave because your mother said it would kill her. How can you not understand me now?"

"That was another time," my mother says, her eyes brimming. "Not like now. Being apart won't be forever. And this way, we'll see you more often."

Pola's eyes widen. Her face is a landscape over which storm clouds have gathered, casting deep shadows.

"What?! How can you say that after what you put us through?" Her voice rises like an air raid siren gearing up.

For a moment, my mother scrambles to recover, summoning her sternest look. With all her power she levels it at Pola. The look says: Bite your tongue.

Before heading to university, I took a detour out of high school and into a job as a teller for the Royal Bank of Canada. I would probably have foregone any further formal education, but I knew I needed it if I wanted to land a good job, the kind my mother said I would likely never get. I hadn't chosen a profession, but I was steadfast in my determination never to learn shorthand, teach, or take care of sick people, not since so much of my childhood had been spent learning to take care of my parents when they were sick.

What I wanted most was to travel. To do that, I needed to earn money, something for which I had a talent. Growing up, the family's finances were always precarious, so I learned not to ask my parents for money. In their tailor shop, my parents worked six days a week, but it was my mother who kept our small family afloat and held the purse strings. Asking my mother for money would have given her too much ammunition.

Israel was not my first choice as a destination but I knew my mother could not object after a lifetime of pouring Zionist propaganda into my ear. Israel was also where my Aunt Tzippah lived and two aunts were all I had, Chana in Argentina and Tzippah in the Promised Land. Family, what was left of it, was on the top of my mother's list of things I needed to experience, right alongside visiting Eretz Israel. Although she was a staunch Zionist, who, in the late 1930s, had hoped to settle there with her new husband, my mother never made it to Israel. Her mother begged her not to leave Poland. When World War II broke out, they were forced to flee to the USSR, leaving my grandmother behind. In the end, it was the Germans who killed my grandmother. And in Trans-Siberia, where life was hard, my mother's husband succumbed to influenza and died. The way I saw it, *not* choosing Palestine is what had really killed him. And in the end, Mankeh, my mother, lost the two people she had loved the most.

At the bank, I managed to save half of my meager salary, greatly impressing my mother who often said how it was good that I had a talent for making money, since I had no talent whatsoever for saving it. It was all worth it, I knew, the moment I heard the umbilical cord stretch and finally snap as the door of the plane was sealed. It was my first flight, my first time out alone in the world, but I only thought about it that way later. At the time, it was all about my mother.

Lod Airport was hot and clamorous. I heard my name being called as I came through the gate, but looking out, I recognized no faces. In my purse was a worn photograph of my Israeli family taken at somebody's *simcha*, but I knew it would bear no resemblance to anyone in the surging crowd before me. Suddenly, it didn't matter as I was engulfed in a sea of outstretched arms, my face was crushed into an ample bosom, thinly covered by a damp blouse. I felt myself drawn into the center, like Dorothy into the vortex of the tornado that dropped her in Oz. My name was being chanted in four-part harmony. *Leah, Leah, Leah, Leee-aaah.* I would have happily responded but for a mouthful of wet fabric. Eventually, Pola, who was holding me firmly around the shoulders, introduced herself, then her husband, her children, Yosef and Tamar, and finally, my Aunt Tzippah, Pola's mother. At seventy, Aunt Tzippah may have been tiny, but she had an unmistakable air of authority. After planting wet kisses on my cheeks and mouth, she grasped me firmly by the elbow, executed an about face, and announced to her family, "*Kuhm* . . . let's go!" As they trailed dutifully behind, Aunt Tzippah led me out of the building and into the blinding sunlight of a late June morning in Tel Aviv.

Years later, I would recall those first impressions as slides I might have seen in an old fashioned Viewmaster. CLICK. A cluster of palm trees (*not potted but growing in the ground*). CLICK. People swarming in the street at three o'clock in the afternoon. (*Doesn't anybody work?*) CLICK. A bus with people piling on in a crush (*So unlike the orderly queues I had witnessed in the London airport*). CLICK. An elderly Hassid precariously perched on a scooter, zooming by, his fringes flying beneath his dark jacket, his wide-brimmed black hat jammed down securely on his head.

All around me, voices were raised stridently conversing in that annoyingly animated way Jews talk. I flinched. Memories of sitting on the bus in Montréal. *Do they have to be so loud?* Then somewhat ashamed, I realized it didn't matter. There was no one here to judge these loud Jews because everyone in the street was Jewish. For the first time in my life, I lost my sense of being alien. These were "my" people, just like my mother had always said. *Wherever you go, if there is a Jew, you will find shelter.* That's what my mother had drummed into me. *We only have each other.*

In the kitchen, my mother and cousins are so silent I can hear the clock ticking.

"Pola, please don't be angry," I implore. "My mother was just trying to cheer you up." But Pola refuses to lift her eyes. Instead, two angry red spots begin to spread across her high cheekbones where some tears still lie. For once, I am having trouble reading my mother's expression. Something has transpired here that I cannot fathom.

With clenched teeth and hooded eyes, Pola repeats, "How could *you*, you of all people, tell me I must let go of my daughter? You know . . . "

"Pola, there's no need to dig up old bones," my mother says quickly, trying again to silence her niece with a look. But Pola refuses to respond.

"We are getting ready for a *simcha*. Your daughter will be married tomorrow. What could be a happier occasion than that?"

Pola glares at my mother. "He came every day to the house for weeks—months—asking why she didn't write!"

By the end of my first week in Israel, I had met all of Tamar's *chaverim*, her circle of friends. The Israelis quickly took to her "American cousin" and I soon relaxed in their ready acceptance. At home, I had always found Israelis a little too boastful and cocky, but now I saw that outside their country they were like a quote out of context. In Israel, I too was out of context, but somehow with a positive result. Back home in Montréal, I had often felt alien, out of sync with North America and at cross purposes with a culture that held no place for me and my European upbringing unless I chose to conform. In Israel, at least, I was exotic. Within a week, I had a suitor.

Micael's family was originally from France and so being

from Québec gave us some common ground. I laughed when my aunt said she didn't like me going out with a black Jew. I laughed, but said nothing. I had learned not to question my aunt.

"What does she mean, a black Jew?" I asked Tamar.

"She means he's Sephardic," explained Tamar, "not Ashkenazi like us."

"But that's silly," said I. "We're all Jews. What's the difference? And besides, we're just dating; we're not getting married."

Tamar had shrugged the whole thing off, but it had me wondering if my mother could have been wrong.

After dating for a couple of weeks, Micael grew a little too familiar one night and my defences went up. I pushed him away. After two days of silence, he called to invite me out again, to the movies. When I accepted, he announced that I would have to pay for both our tickets. It *was* 1966 and I didn't mind going Dutch, but this was something else. I said I didn't pay to date boys. He told me the date was off. I put down the receiver without saying goodbye.

That night, Tamar and I joined the crowd at My Mother's Eyebrow, an old villa in Yafo perched high on a cliff overlooking the Mediterranean. I walked in through the large double doors a few steps behind Tamar, who shimmied and shook her way across the dance floor of the large room, greeting people all along the way. The floor was brightly lit and rimmed with café tables and chairs, tucked invitingly into the shadowed corners. At the back, four large French doors opened onto a wide terrace with a view of the sea. Tamar's friends had bunched some tables, and were sitting together, talking and smoking. Every once in a while someone would address me in English to include me in the conversation, but I didn't mind being on the fringe, observing, and when Tamar tried to drag me onto the dance floor and into the crush of bodies, I pulled away saying I was content to sit on the sidelines.

Scanning the room, I spotted Alex, one of Tamar's friends and one of the few chaverim who spoke English fluently. Alex was standing in a small group being entertained by a handsome joker who was holding his audience enthralled, telling a story in a variety of voices and exaggerated movements. Easing smoothly from one character into another, he built the story to a crescendo that left everyone rolling with laughter. Several arms reached out in congratulations, clapping the storyteller on the back; he slowly turned and looked nonchalantly in my direction. Catching my eyes on him, though, he quickly turned back and began speaking animatedly to Alex. After a moment, Alex headed my way wearing a conspiratorial smile, and I was surprised to feel the heat rising in my face.

"Leah, someone would like to meet you, but we aren't sure if you're waiting for Micael," said Alex.

"I'm not waiting for Micael," I answered, "not tonight or any night."

"Oh, that's good . . . I mean, Moshe over there would like to meet you."

"You mean the clown?" I hadn't meant it to come out like that, but Alex seemed not to notice.

"Well, yeah, Moshe is a funny guy—if you know what he's saying—a really great guy. I'll bring him over. Yeah? Okay?" I nodded and pulled a duMaurier from the pack on the table to give my hands something to do. I put the cigarette in my mouth and lit it slowly. When I looked up, it was into a tanned, lean face with deep-set, dark brown eyes.

"Ah, Virginia tobacco," Moshe said. I smiled, offering him the pack, but he shook his head, pulling out a package of Time cigarettes from his shirt pocket. He cocked his head and gave me a small, crooked smile as if to say that he preferred his own. I thought I had never seen such perfectly even, white teeth before. I wished, as I often did, that I could become invisible. I wanted to scrutinize him more carefully but without giving myself away. Now close up, he seemed so serious, not like a clown at all. It was the eyes, I decided while I waited for him to say something. But he just stood there, looking down at me, smiling that crooked smile and suddenly it occurred to me that perhaps he couldn't speak any English. A little ache, like a hunger pang, tugged at a string inside me.

"Why don't you sit down?" I said, gesturing. He pulled up a chair opposite me and finally said, "Hallo . . . I am Moshe Almozlino."

"Shalom," I said, suddenly shy. "My name is Leah, Leah Smilovitz. My brother's second name is Moshe," I said, then felt foolish.

He looked at me and seemed about to speak, but his eyes clouded over. He turned sharply to Alex and erupted in a burst of Hebrew. Alex smiled wryly and turned to me.

"Moshe says he hopes you don't mind if I translate for him. His English isn't very good. He says that he has seen you here before and was hoping for the chance to meet you." Alex looked over at Moshe who began speaking again in a rush, then stopped short, as if holding back a team of runaway horses.

"He says he hopes that he is not being too . . . " Alex groped for a word, "intimate . . . like rude. No, that's not it, but you know what I mean, because he knows that you have been seeing Micael but he thinks Micael is not good for a girl like you."

I looked up with some surprise at the handsome face across from me—what a nice face, I thought—and spoke to Alex without once taking my eyes off Moshe.

"Tell him not to worry. Tell him he's right about Micael; he's not good for me."

As Alex translated, Moshe's face broke into a wide grin. I could feel my color rise again. Our translator waited patiently for someone to speak, looking from one to the other, then, with a shrug, Alex turned and walked away. His departure went unnoticed. At the back of the disco, the jukebox began to play an old favorite. Moshe's smile grew wider as he stood and held out his hand. He began to sing in a soft low voice, *"Oh-oh, yes I'm the great pretender."*

I laughed at his perfect phrasing, his sudden ability to express himself in English. He put his arms around my waist and moved me onto the dance floor.

"Pretending that I'm doing well . . . La-la lala, la-la lala . . . I'm lonely but no one can tell," he sang to me. We danced into the middle of the floor. Tenderly, he rested his chin against the side of my head. His arms draped themselves on my hips, but his body, hard and lean, kept its distance as we danced through one song and into another.

Slow dancing was made for discovery. I felt comfortable in the circle of his arms, suddenly serene. In just a few moments, my guard had fallen and surprisingly, there were no signals warning me to raise it again.

Perhaps because I had not learned English until I was four, I had always been vigilant about language. For me, it was a sharp tool that required attention. To accurately convey meaning, to cut to the core of things, to avoid inflicting any accidental wounds, for all these reasons and more, words must be used with precision. Still, I had always known it was dangerous to take anything, especially myself, too seriously. I learned that self-deprecating humor was an excellent defence against my mother's demands or the sexual hunger of young men. But with Moshe, I was rendered speechless. Not having to measure and weigh my words—or his—I was at once protected and naked. We soon invented a language of our own.

"Who came to the house every day?" I ask.

My mother fires a fierce look at Pola, accompanied by an index finger held rigid in its mixture of fury and self-control. Pola's lower lip is trembling, her jaw line taut. The silence in the kitchen has been stretched unbearably thin, like skin over a boil.

"Pola?" My mother says in a voice so strangulated, I look to see if she isn't choking. Sometimes she suffers from attacks of nerves that leave her face and neck drained of blood, but this is not now the case. In fact, her color is high, her face is glistening and her eyes are bright, little stones.

"Mameh, what's going on?" I ask, keeping my voice low. It trembles and there's a queasy feeling circling in the pit of my stomach. I have spent a lifetime learning to read my mother like a barometer, adapting myself to the swift changes of her moods and emotions. But I've never seen her like this, wavering between fear and uncertainty.

"Nothing is going on," says my mother. "Pola's just upset about Tamar getting married and moving so far away. Right, Pola?"

The vacuum of silence turns me away from my mother to look down at Pola who is not moving, not even breathing. Her eyes are nailed to a particular spot on the tablecloth.

"Pola? Who came to the house every day?" I repeat with as much control as I can muster.

"Tell her," Tamar squawks, unable to bear the pressure on her mother for one more moment. "Tell her how Moshe came every day, looking for a letter."

"Moshe?" My voice is a hoarse croak, as I summon him from the world of the dead.

He came to the Bat Yam beach every afternoon to see me as soon as the shop where he worked closed for siesta. He was an electrician, in the employ of an uncle. My Aunt Tzippah, however, was unimpressed with both his profession and his address. She wanted more details on his family, but sitting on the beach, Moshe and I had better things to discuss. We somehow wiled away the hours teaching each other new words and laughing as if the summer was endless. At four o'clock, he would return to work with the promise of seeing me again at eight.

In Israel, social life only really began at nine in the evening, after supper, when people spilled out of their apartments and onto the streets, down the boulevards, and into the cafés and squares. Accustomed to the North American habit of saving all socializing for the weekend, I was dumbfounded by the swarm of people out on a Monday night. It was this joy of being on the street, despite the barrier of language, that made me feel at home. My mother said that Israel was built as a home for us all. Wouldn't she be proud that I had become something of a Zionist? I wrote my parents a letter telling them how happy I was in Israel and, of course, all about Moshe.

One day, my aunt suggested to Pola that Moshe should be invited to join the family for Shabbat. I was anxious to introduce him to my aunt and thought Pola must have put in a good word. She had already told me how much they thought Moshe was a real *mensche*, a good and honest soul. I wanted my family to like him, but I was not yet ready to admit it meant anything. I was afraid to make something too meaningful of this summer romance. And yet, he was so different from any boy I had ever known.

The eldest of two sons, he had lost his father when he was eleven and had begun to work as soon as he was bar mitzvahed so as to relieve some of the burden on his mother. His uncle had taken him in seven years ago as an apprentice, and Moshe had worked long and hard to win his approval. His brother, younger by five years, wanted to be a doctor and Moshe knew without being told that the onus would fall on him to support the family until then.

All the things that seemed important back home when I had been going steady with Sam were non-issues between me and Moshe, especially the matter of sex, which Moshe was very cautious about, never pressing for favors and sometimes, being the one to pull away when our kisses grew too deep.

Tamar had teased me all day Friday about the fuss I was making over the impending family dinner. "I promise you," Tamar gave her throaty guffaw, "right after we greet the Shabbat as queen, we'll treat your Moshe like a king."

"I'm not worried about you and your parents. It's Tzippah I'm scared of."

What I feared was the inevitable interrogation I knew Moshe would have to face. It seemed I would always be under the control of censoring females. I knew the process was necessary, although I was not yet prepared to admit for what purpose.

"Aah! My grandmother Tzippah needs to investigate. She knows everyone who knows everyone who lives in the old town," Tamar proudly boasted. "The Mossad doesn't have such a powerful network. If there's something to learn about the Almozlino *mishpochah* of Yafo, we will know it in forty-eight hours, I promise you."

My aunt proved cordial, even warm towards Moshe, seeming to take immediately to his quiet charm and good looks. The Shabbat meal was the biggest of the week, and after all the formalities and endless courses, we sat digesting, elbows planted on the table, ready to tackle the serious business of politics and gossip, which in Israel were interchangeable. Despite the endless barrage of questions my aunt fired at him, Moshe remained at ease and unruffled. He only grew restive when Yosef talked about his impending tour of duty, the one month each year that every Israeli male was obliged to serve in the army. All in all, though, things had gone well and by the time it was all over, I imagined I saw my seventy-year-old aunt blatantly flirting with my boyfriend.

Afterward, Moshe and I sauntered over to the park across the street and sat on a bench. The full moon was huge. It looked as ripe and juicy as a melon. Gazing at it, I wished I could take a big bite, let the juice run down my arms to the elbows, let the sweet meat cool my mouth. Moshe had draped one arm around my shoulders and with the other, held my hand lightly. Lazy as a cat, he leaned over and nuzzled my neck, burying his face beneath my thick, auburn hair. He flicked his tongue playfully and licked the sweat from the hollow at the base of my skull. A shiver slipped down my spine. I leaned into him, and with eyes closed, sought his mouth with the taste of the moon still on my tongue.

The kiss was soft, so gentle that it lodged a low ache beneath my breastbone. Hungrily, I pulled him closer, wanting to fill the hollow that was growing so quickly in me, it hurt. He kissed me harder, then pulled his mouth away and buried it once again in my hair. Holding me tightly, he said, "*Ani ohev otach*. I love you, Leah."

I remained still, looking at the moon over his shoulder.

"Leah?" he said, uncertainty creeping into his voice.

"Shhh," I said, "I am savoring this moment to remember my whole life long."

He loved me. No one had ever said they loved me before,

except in response. So eager was I for love, I had always been the first to blurt out those words. With this one sweet sentence, Moshe had given me the greatest gift.

"*Ani ohev otach*," I finally replied. And Moshe laughed. "Ahh, you want to say *ani ohevet otcha*. I am man, for woman you say another way."

We laughed and hugged. And he kissed me until I was so dizzy I would have danced naked beneath the juicy moon or slipped unnoticed into his pocket so he could take me home. But instead, he walked me to the arbor for one last embrace. The buses didn't run on the Sabbath and it was a long walk back to Yafo. Pulling away after one last kiss, he placed his open palm on the side of my cheek and for the second time that night told me, "Ani ohev otach."

"I love you too, Moshe." More than I ever imagined possible.

On the beach the next day, we sat cross-legged opposite one another while Tamar had a rousing game of *matkot*, paddle ball, with Alex who had become our almost constant companion during the last month. I suddenly remembered the look that had darkened Moshe's face the night before and asked, "Why were you so upset yesterday when Yosef talked about returning to the army for his duty?"

"Ahh, yes. You know, it is hard for my mother when I go to the army. I must to go in the fall but I try now to make special . . . uhhh . . . I ask for . . ."

"An exemption?"

"Yes. I want they should let me stay home because there is not enough money in the house without me."

"You are so good to your family."

"They need me, Leah," Moshe said, his voice dropping as if telling me a secret, "but I also afraid that someday I go in the army and not come home. I hate it. I think, sometimes I will die in the army."

"What about Moshe?"

I am sitting down now; my leg bones have suddenly melted away. The question hangs in the still air as I look from Tamar to Pola to my mother. Still, no one speaks. We are all frozen like actors in a movie with a stalled projector.

I ask again, "What about Moshe? What do you mean he came for months after, looking for a letter?" I ask, even as a terrible reality begins taking shape in the silence that is filling with the ghostly apparition of a handsome young man. Only the sound of my own voice keeps the ghost at bay, a voice that has suddenly grown shrill.

"What do you mean he came for months afterwards? How could he come to your house, Pola, if . . . ?"

Moshe arrived at breakfast the Tuesday following his dinner with us and much to my surprise and delight, I learned that we had the whole day to spend together.

"Is it a holiday today?" I asked, surprised no one had mentioned it.

"A holiday?" He looked puzzled, then smiled, "Yes, yes, a holiday for Leah and Moshe. We play hockey."

"Hockey?"

I thought for a moment and then laughed, "You mean hooky. We are going to take the day off without permission."

Hand in hand, we rode the Egged bus into downtown Tel Aviv and headed straight for a favorite haunt, the Brechot Gordon, the saltwater swimming pool near the Sheraton. It opened early and we were among the first in, finding a good spot where we could settle in for a day of luxurious idleness. We had brought a large bottle of *miz tapozim*, grapefruit juice, to prevent dehydration and lots of suntan oil. It was good to be alone. We had grown so accustomed to always having Alex or Tamar around that we almost hadn't noticed we no longer needed translators to communicate. I was glad also to be able to tell Moshe in private that the word had come back from my aunt that the Almozlinos had a very good reputation and that Moshe, in particular, had been cited for his devotion to family and ability to earn a living. All this I relayed with some degree of embarrassment as I still found the "investigation" to be outlandish and intrusive. I did not mention that my aunt had also said that she had liked Moshe despite the fact that he was almost a black Jew having come as he did from Bulgarian stock. Bulgarians, it seemed were a gray area, somewhere between Ashkenazi and Sephardim. Apparently, Moshe was a gray Jew. Despite my discomfort, Moshe received the news with enthusiasm, grinning broadly, his perfectly even teeth gleaming impossibly white in a deeply tanned face. He had been waiting to hear just this but had been afraid to ask. Now, sitting on the straw mat facing me, he took both of my hands into his and said, "Do not go home."

I laughed lightly. "What do you mean?" wanting and not wanting to hear his reply.

"I want you to stay in Israel, to stay with me. Do not go home. If you stay, you can take Ulpan and learn Hebrew. You can find work because you are smart and we can be married when I come back from the army."

I was feeling giddy. Not go home. Not return to Montréal, to my mother, to my father and brother. Not return to begin university where a deposit had been made for my first year; to my friends; to "sometimes Sam;" to the Leah I had been—and would never be again.

"I don't know," I began.

"You love me, no?" he asked and I nodded, yes, yes, yes, but there were so many strings attached to those words, all of them leading to a complicated tangle of explanations. There was no direct line, I knew, between "Yes, I love you" and "No, I can't stay." An ocean of reasons lay between them and yet, here I was. Fate had brought us together. Would fate not keep us that way? I cast around for an explanation about what I was feeling.

"If I don't go home now, my mother will be terribly upset. She depends on me, Moshe. There are times when I am everything to her. I can't leave her without some preparation. It could kill her, Moshe."

He nodded slowly, his smile fading, a deep crease forming between his brows. He understood family obligations. He understood that what seemed so simple, would not be so easy after all. Nothing ever was. So with our obligations clearly outlined, we began to talk tentatively, seriously, about what the alternatives were. By the end of the day, we had charted a course that was reasonable and acceptable. I would return home to attend university. Moshe would work double shifts, if he could, to make extra money. I would take Hebrew as an elective course; maybe do well enough to apply for a position with a North American company before returning. He would likely do his tour of duty with the army. Most important of all, I would write him every week and he would write as often as he could get Alex or Tamar to help him. I would be back in May, just nine months away, and we would be married that summer. By the end of the day, we realized that we hadn't eaten, so engrossed had we been in laying out our future.

From that moment on, the lightheartedness of our early days seemed to vanish. Summer was running out. As my departure date drew closer, Moshe grew more anxious with each day, showing up even during working hours to steal whatever moments he could. And it was taking its toll on him, but he refused to miss even one night with me. "There will be plenty of time to sleep when you go home," he said sadly. "Then I will sleep long, because only in my dreams will I be able to see you."

My flight was scheduled for eleven p.m. and despite my protests, Moshe insisted that he would accompany me on the bus to Lod Airport along with Pola and Tamar. I, too, was exhausted. In my mind, I had been playing out, in endless variations, a scene where I announce to my parents that I am in love and will be moving to Israel to marry Moshe. In all the versions I envisioned, not one ended well. I knew, whatever I did, my job would be to convince my parents that this was where my happiness lay. My father would be sad but supportive; it was my mother I feared telling. But this was what I wanted, what fate had handed me—a gift, the heart of a man who will wait for me patiently more than nine thousand miles away. It would be hard to convince them, but if they truly loved me, I reasoned, they would only want my happiness and it was Moshe who had made me happier than I had ever been.

Later, what I would remember of our final moments and the bus ride to the airport was that somehow Moshe scratched his gum and it bled, so that when he turned and smiled bravely at me, a little red line of blood trickled down his front teeth. I reached up and kissed him, wiping his teeth clean with my tongue. The metallic taste of blood remained in my mouth for awhile. In the end, we were all in tears, including Pola and Tamar. I wondered what would happen if I did not get on the plane. Would my mother go wild with grief? With fury? What was the worst that could happen? How could I leave him like this? How could I not go home? Conflicted, I boarded the plane.

My parents took my news with surprisingly little opposition. I waited for my mother's histrionics, but it was my father who seemed the most agitated. Maybe he feared losing his one ally in his endless squabbles with my mother. She calmed him by saying that their little girl was grown up now and entitled to have a life of her own choosing. In all the scenarios I had played out in my head, my mother had never emerged as an advocate for my departure. Totally disarmed in that first week after my return, I sat with her for hours recounting all the things I had done, what Moshe was like, and the life I had witnessed in Israel. And my mother seemed to drink it all in. I thought we had never been so close.

As I had promised, I wrote Moshe every week, although getting organized for university immediately upon my return had been a shock to the system. It surprised me, though, how easily I slipped back into the rhythm. It was all made easier as my mother went out of her way to be helpful.

With great excitement, I received the first letter in the form of a New Year's card that said:

"Shana Tova. Happy New Year. I hope it will be as short as posible. Moshe"

It made me laugh and I wrote him a long letter telling him all about school and my Hebrew professor who was Greek, of all things, and how my parents were not happy, but had accepted that I would be moving to Israel. When my mother saw the letter to Moshe on the dresser, she asked if I needed a stamp and if I wanted it mailed right away.

It felt so good to finally be acknowledged as an adult. It was clear to me that I had made the right decision in coming home, facing my parents, giving them the respect that was their due. I felt a new bond with my mother. Perhaps I *was* going to live the life that she had been denied, and for once, I wasn't trying to avoid it.

The second letter I received from Moshe was much longer.

15.9.66

Dear Leah!
I just get your lovely letter, so I am writing you for remainding how much I love you.

I did'nt write you before because no body wanted to writh it for me, I begd Alex sometimes but he always said that he haven't time.

I begin to wait for you, it will be a long, long year but I am shure that nothing will change my mind about us.

I LOVE you Leah and I always will. Althow the short time we have together, I think I know you enoth to love you.

Leah, I mise you, so much that I thought about you all the time. Afether our dayly meetings, I feel now empty. I mise something, something I love, I mise you.

This letter is my first it is short but I hope it teles you everything I fill about you.

I am waiting to your next letter and hope you will send me in it the pictures we have on the beach.

For ever my love,
Moshe
P.S. Writh your letters clearly please

It was the last letter I was to receive. Although I continued to write, nothing came back. After a month, I thought that perhaps with two jobs and trying to get Alex to help him write, it must be difficult. Every day, I asked my mother if I had any mail and always, the answer was no. My mother said not to worry, that certainly a letter would come soon. Moshe's tour of duty was scheduled to begin in mid-October. Two months passed with no word.

By mid-November, I began to imagine he had changed his mind and said as much in a long angst-filled letter to Tamar. I asked that she check around; see if perhaps he had a new girlfriend. Maybe I had just been a summer fling. Maybe he had been playing games. Anything was possible when there was nothing but awful silence upon which to project my fears.

On December 1, my mother silently handed me a letter

from Israel. It was from Tamar and uncharacteristically, my mother left me alone to read it. Tamar said that she had bad news. It seems Moshe had been on his tour of duty near the Golan Heights. He was to relieve a friend of his on guard duty and decided to play a little joke. He put on a white headdress and called out to his friend. He was shot through the heart, Tamar wrote, before he could identify himself with the password.

I could not cry. I read the letter over and over again but could not cry. He could not be dead. I would have known if he was dead, I would have felt something, I was certain of it. But there had been no letters. No word since mid-September. Later, I was unable to recall shedding any tears for Moshe. I just buried him quietly somewhere near to my solar plexus.

My mother appeared sympathetic but relieved that I was holding myself together. Two weeks later, my father suffered a heart attack. My mother said it was because he had worried so much about losing me. It had weakened him.

"He's not a strong man, you know," I had heard my mother repeat to friends and neighbors over and over again. Six weeks later, while visiting my father in the convalescent home, I met Danny and a year later, we were married.

"Tell me now," I say louder than I intend. "Tell me everything. I must know everything . . . I have a right to know,

now that you have unearthed the dead. You owe it to me. Tell me—EVERYTHING!" My face is hot and my eyes are stinging, but I will not cry.

I look over at my mother who is about to speak and for the first time in my life, I feel not one ounce of emotion. Neither love nor hate; not compassion nor anger. I barely recognize her at all.

"Tell me about Moshe," I address Pola, forcing myself to be calm. "What do you think I will do? Leave Danny and run off to Israel to find Moshe? It's been six years. Too much has changed for the clock to be turned back, so please, you must tell me everything."

Pola finally looks up at me and says, "He came every day, every day from the day you left and for months afterwards. It was my mother, your Aunt Tzippah. She didn't think he was good enough for you, just an electrician, she said. And Mankeh, your mother, was driving us *mishuggah* with letters saying we must do something to stop you from ruining your life. Even before you left, we knew that you would not come back.

"He stopped coming when we told him you were going to be married," Pola says, lowering her eyes, finally shamed by the look on my stricken face.

"But my letters? Didn't he receive . . . ?"

In a flash, I understand—how many times my mother had so helpfully offered to mail my letters, how she always had been the first to get the mail, sometimes intercepting the postman. Why had I been so willing to believe that my mother would let me go?

Now, it is obvious why my efforts had been so futile when I tried to convince my parents to allow me to become a volunteer during the Six Day War. My mother's refusal was not out of fear that I might be hurt, but that I might learn Moshe was not dead. My mother had panicked, convinced I would learn to what extent she had been willing to go to keep me bound to her.

"Why, Mameh?" I ask. "Why did you do this to me?"

"I could not let you go," she says without a hint of remorse. "It would have killed me."

TATEH AND THE ANGEL OF DEATH
A FAMILY FABLE

WHEN I WAS A LITTLE GIRL, Tateh and I would go fishing. There were the rituals—stripping a young birch to make a pole, digging for worms, and walking through woods to the river—all made sweeter for taking place beyond the range of my squalling baby brother and my mother's vigilant eye. I could run along the bank of the river in search of the perfect spot to drop our lines and never once hear a cautionary note escape my father's smiling lips. Unlike my mother, my Tateh had no dire predictions about reckless behavior and entertained no anxiety over what one false step might bring. Not that my father was the fearless type. Later on, I would speculate that he only taught me how to fish so I would be the one to hook the worm.

As we sat on the grassy riverbank, hugging our knees and our poles, waiting for a tug that came only rarely, my father would tell me stories, wonderful Russian fables about talking fish and how the vain bear was tricked by the jealous fox into losing his bushy tail. And sometimes Tateh told my favorite story about how on three separate occasions, and with God's help, he had cheated the Angel of Death.

When my Tateh was an infant, my grandmother, Muschia, undertook an arduous journey by foot and by cart from Baranowicze in Byelorussia to Vilna in Lithuania. The year was 1911. Just months before, my grandfather, Moishe, had been conscripted into the czar's army, leaving his wife to care for their two adolescent daughters, beloved baby son, and their little farm outside Baranowicze. While in the service of the czar, my grandfather would contract consumption and over time, the illness would wear him down the way he wore down the nibs of his pens as he copied out tracts of Torah. But in 1911, it was her son, not her husband, that Muschia feared losing.

The child had contracted rheumatic fever. For a week, Muschia and her young daughters did what they could, but despite all efforts, the little boy was burning up. The doctor said nothing more could be done, but Muschia refused to accept the prognosis. There was one last hope for saving her son. She would make a pilgrimage to consult a *tzaddik*, a righteous man renowned for his understanding of the mysteries of this world and the next. She was a practical woman, my Tateh said, leaving the mysteries of the world to her husband and all the men who studied Torah. Moishe spent his days copying brief tracts of scripture onto parchment in a miniature hand. Each tiny scroll copied would be placed inside a *mezzuzah*, like a soul inhabiting a body, and each would find its way to the right side of some Jewish doorway. Muschia feared for her son, feared that his soul might leave his fevered body. Already there were four tiny coffins in the cemetery, each holding the body of a son, dead and buried by the age of two. The child who would become my father had just turned two when he fell ill.

Determined, Muschia left the fevered child in the hands of her capable daughters. After a day's journey, my grandmother wearily arrived at the rabbi's court in Vilna. She sat waiting for almost an entire day and was finally ushered into the inner chamber. There the tzaddik listened to Muschia's straightforward tale of four dead and one dying son.

When she finished, he told her he needed time to reflect and pray, that she should return the following morning. On the next day, the tzaddik gave his advice.

"You must trick the Angel of Death. That will keep your young son from being taken."

Dismayed, my grandmother asked how she was supposed to do that.

"All things are possible," the tzaddik told her, "when there is an Almighty to guide us. To trick the *malaach hamuvet*, we must change the name your son was given at his *bris*."

Muschia had never heard of such a thing, and asked bluntly if it was allowed.

The tzaddik assured her that it was not so uncommon in Galicia where he came from.

"But by what name should I call him?" she asked.

"Benzion. You must call him Son of Zion, and the Angel of Death will pass him by," said the tzaddik, thus ending the audience that changed my father's name and saved his life.

There is an old Yiddish anecdote about a man whose birth, bar mitzvah, wedding, and funeral took place in four different countries although he never left his home town. So it was for my father. Born in Czarist Russia, my Tateh was bar mitzvahed, apprenticed as a tailor, and married in Poland. And some ten years later, he rejoiced at the arrival of his third child and only son, born to him in the USSR. In all that time, my father never once left Baranowicze, not until 1941, two years after his son's birth. That was the year Hitler turned on his Soviet allies and began the march on Moscow. It was then that the Bolsheviks came to conscript my father, just as some thirty years before, his father had been conscripted into the Czar's Imperial Army.

TATEH AND THE ANGEL OF DEATH

"We lived in a place that never belonged to anyone for long," my Tateh said.

Before 1917, Byelorussia had been part of the Czarist Empire, but in 1920, after more than a century, it was once again returned to Poland. Then in 1939, the Germans handed over western Byelorussia to the Soviets as a reward for their alliance with the Axis.

The Soviets were fierce and ruthless, my father said. Soon the Jews of Baranowicze prayed for the Germans to replace them. After all, my father recounted, his eyes downcast, everyone knew that the Germans were a civilized people and the Russians, pigs. It would seem that in my father's town, there was not much news of the ghettos that were spreading like malignant cells throughout Eastern Europe, nothing about the rounding up of Jews like cattle, or of transports and concentration camps. No papers carried such news in the USSR. No fleeing Jews passed through with tales of horror. Or maybe, the stories were told in Baranowicze but were not believed, as so often was the case.

"Who would have believed such a thing?" my Tateh asked.

When my father protested to the commandant of the unit that he had three children, a wife, and a mother all depending on him to protect them, he was assured that the Germans were interested only in men to people their forced labor camps. Women and children were safe from the Germans. That's what they told him and that's what he had to believe.

So the Soviets handed my father a rifle as he kissed his family good-bye. Hands that had never held anything larger than shears for cutting cloth, fingers talented enough to sew a stitch that magically disappeared, and eyes trained to measure a form perfectly were now expected to draw a bead on the enemy, pull the trigger, and cut him down. My father was now required to make Germans magically disappear into the folds of the earth as if they were stitches in cloth.

Perhaps having been raised by three women, my father was uneasy in the company of men. He never spoke of men as friends, not even in stories about his childhood. He admitted to *a shvacheh neshomeh*, a soft nature. But if his were hands that could not kill, they were hands that could sew and, in the end, that was what would save him.

They were on foot and heading to Moscow, my father said. It was bitterly cold. The wind howled constantly, swirling across frozen fields as the ragtag army marched, their makeshift uniforms flapping wildly as if waving goodbye to all they had ever known. My father's fingers were frozen and his shoulder ached from carrying the heavy rifle. His head ached too, from the wind biting at his face and the relentless glare off the snowfields. In advance of the men, the colonel mounted on horseback, was moving ahead slowly.

Looking up, wondering what it would be like to be on the back of an animal, my father's boot struck a rock. He tripped, lost his balance, and fell forward, clutching desperately at his rifle. It flew from his hands, arced into the air and landed butt down with such force that it went off. And it killed the colonel's horse out from under him.

My father's execution was set for sunrise.

That night, the colonel raged about the stupidity of soldiers who could not even hold onto a rifle. The colonel's wife, a captain in the company, listened with half an ear as her husband vented his fury over losing a perfectly good horse at the hands of a fumbling tailor, a Jew, no less. Perhaps, the colonel's wife looked up, but slowly, so as not to convey too much interest.

"A tailor?" she may have said. "If only he knew how to sew a decent uniform for you."

In this manner, as my father told it, she convinced the colonel that a live tailor might make up, in some small way, for a dead horse. And that is how my father slipped past the Angel of Death a second time. When she came to see him in his cell, my father said, the colonel's wife confided that she too was a Jew, but warned him to hold his tongue and prove himself an excellent tailor, for she would not defend him again. There was no need for her to worry. Apprenticed at fourteen, my father had a gift with cloth and an eye for design. He could cut a pattern merely by studying a photo or a garment. So, after the necessary materials were liberated somehow, my father successfully produced a new uniform for the colonel and, out of gratitude, a dress for the colonel's wife. The memory of her pleasure would prove invaluable on another occasion.

As it happened, before my father's battalion could reach Moscow, it was redirected to the eastern front. They marched or sat crammed onto trains whenever their route intersected the railway lines. My father no longer carried a gun but to compensate, he had been loaded down with additional supplies. Sometimes, waiting at a station for trains that ran on erratic schedules, he would steal some sleep in a quiet corner. That's how he came to be left behind. Separated from his battalion, my father haunted the station for two days until he finally connected with another troop. They found him wandering about with a small but precious cache of goods. He was immediately branded a deserter. Deserters were summarily shot, but that was not to be my father's fate. He remembered how the colonel's wife had loved her dress. So, overcoming his fear, he asked to speak with the commandant and suggested that perhaps there was some woman for whom the officer might like to make a fine present of a lovely warm dress or even a coat. The commandant was willing and my father wily enough to trade a few small possessions for some fabric. With the needle, thread, thimble and shears he now always carried in his greatcoat, my Tateh cut and sewed his escape from death yet again.

But the Angel came looking for him during the war one last time.

TATEH AND THE ANGEL OF DEATH

They were marching, always marching, my father said. It was early in the winter of 1943 and food supplies were as meager as the memory of spring. The band of soldiers was hungrier than they had ever been, and exhausted beyond human limits. They encountered few villages and when they did, there was never any food to be found. Still, the unit continued across the barrenness of Trans-Siberia and every day, a few men fell and were left where they lay to die, perhaps to be eaten by wolves whose nightly baying would have been terrifying if the men had not been so numbed by hunger.

On the day my father decided to die, they were marching through a large orchard. The gnarled apple trees standing in neat rows must have seemed a rebuke, a mockery of the ragged formation presented by the struggle of men moving through it. My father dragged his feet, festering with sores from months of living in damp boots. Finally, unable to take another step, he fell against a tree and slid onto the cold, hard ground.

He closed his eyes in exhaustion, in resignation, in the certainty he would not open them again. Perhaps he thought of his wife and children as he had last seen them, crying and frightened, or of his mother who had adored the son whose life she had snatched from the malaach hamuvet.

There beneath the tree, my father fell into the sleep that invites death. And he dreamt. He dreamt that he lay beneath an apple tree in a cold, bleak orchard where bony branches stretched out like the fingers of an arthritic crone. He was alone except for a figure in the distance that seemed to sometimes walk, sometimes float as it made its way toward him. As he watched, my father trembled with fear believing that, at last, the Angel of Death was coming to claim him. But as the figure drew nearer, his heart lightened as he recognized his father, Moishe. He saw the ink-stained fingers gently reach out with longing in what might have been the beginning of a caress. But instead of reaching down to touch his son, Moishe reached up, up and above my father's head to pluck a golden apple from a leafless branch. Then he offered the apple to his son whose arm felt so heavy, he was unable to lift it, even though his mouth had begun to water in anticipation of the first bite. The apple was perfect; its burnished skin shone, glinting in the sun that stood just above and behind my grandfather's shoulder.

"Take it," said my father's father. "Take a big bite, Benzion, my son."

"I am too weak, Tateh," replied my father. "I cannot move and anyway, this is only a dream for you are long dead, may you reside in the heavenly Garden of Eden."

"No, I am here," said Moishe, "and you must eat this apple. For if you eat it all, you will live. And you must live. You are my only son. You must not die here, for if you do, who will say *Kaddish* for me?"

And my father took the apple and ate it. When he awoke, he said, he marched for another day as if renewed, and finally they arrived at a town where there was food enough for all.

Once, when I was old enough to have known better, I made the mistake of referring to my father's escape from the Angel of Death in the presence of my mother. Almost instantly, I felt guilty for having exposed my Tateh to her cynical judgment. She turned to him and said, "You have filled your daughter's head with *narishkeit,* with your nonsense stories and fables. Thank God she has me to tell her the truth."

Fables or truths. Even now, I favor my father's fables, so full of hope, to my mother's ominous truths.

One day when he was seventy, my father lay down for a nap on the cutting table in the backroom of his tailor shop. That table had had many lives. Purchased second-hand when I was a toddler, it served as the dining room table for our little family of four. At Rosh Hashanah and Passover we took our holiday meals on it until my parents bought the tailor shop and then the table took on a new role. At lunch, my father would eat on it the hot meals my mother brought from home. When done, he would clear away the dishes and carefully wipe down the wood before unrolling a bolt of cloth that he would cut into a suit or a dress. But since my mother's death three years earlier, business had dwindled and now the table was mostly used for afternoon naps.

When I called to check on him that day, my Tateh

said he was feeling tired, unable to concentrate on putting the finishing touches to Mrs. Tweedy's jacket. It was only Tuesday and he had promised it for Saturday. He had plenty of time, he reasoned, and then, as if talking to himself, said he had been thinking about Drora. His eldest daughter was ten when he last saw her. Such a good girl, he said. He didn't want to dwell on how she had died, but he was thinking about how the Angel of Death had released her from Auschwitz and delivered her to the radiance of Gan Eden. I grew anxious, perhaps because he rarely mentioned his "other" children, so I drove down to his shop where I found him on the table, lying on his side and clutching his left arm.

In the ambulance, his eyes were closed but his lips were moving. I leaned in closer and took his cool, gnarled hand in mine.

"I can almost see her," he said softly. "The sunlight is on her face and she is calling, 'Tateh, Tateh. I am here. Come, we are all here . . . we're waiting . . .'"

We were rounding the corner to the hospital when my father sighed. His hand slipped from mine. And the Angel of Death led him to the other side.

MISSING IN ACTION

A WARM BREEZE blew in through the car window as I crested the hill on Grosvenor. The sun, red as a giant dahlia, sat perched high on the treetops. The sight of the graceful, old maples set aflame by the slipping sun loosened the tension that had been building in my neck all day. I pulled the car into a spot right at the foot of the walk and had the odd sensation that something was not right. It was the empty spot in front of the house where Danny's new Audi 500 should have been. I grabbed my briefcase, stuffed with work I would ignore as soon as I set foot inside the house. Why I dragged it home every night was a mystery, like

Danny not being home when he insisted we have dinner on time tonight.

M.I.A. Missing In Action.

That's the phrase Danny would have used—had, in fact, used to describe the scene that morning last April when he had discovered his beloved Audi was gone, silently towed away by thieves in the middle of the night. "M.I.A.," he had said.

Actually, what he had said was, "SHIT! DO YOU FUCKIN' BELIEVE THIS? MY AUDI IS M.I.A. Un-fucking-believable . . . to steal a car from right in front of your door. And I didn't hear a thing! ME—me who wakes up if a cat farts a block away!"

"It's only a car," I said, trying to console him. "It's not an arm, a leg, or a person. Your insurance will cover you. There are more important things in life to have apoplexy about."

"That's the sympathy I get?" asked Danny, annoyed.

"If it's sympathy you want, you're barking up the wrong woman, remember? Sympathy's what you got from your girlfriends. You married me for my pragmatism."

I walked into the kitchen and stopped to wonder if Danny had said anything about an errand. Sometimes, when I was deep into what I was doing at the office, Danny would talk and I would nod, even though the only thing to register was that his lips were moving. I somehow trusted my brain to file the information for later use. Sharing an office had turned out to be a mixed blessing. Although Danny always knew where I was, he still didn't understand why I wasn't available to him at all times.

Thinking hard, I stared blankly at the wall and the Wedgwood-blue phone that matched the print I had so meticulously papered the wall with some ten years earlier. It was a happy little print that Danny tolerated. He preferred the walls stark white.

Suddenly, I envisioned him standing face-to-face with his older brother, Beryl, in the cramped hallway of their father's duplex, talking to, but not looking at, one another. A shiver zipped down my spine. I had a sensation that something had happened to my father-in-law. Since my mother-in-law had died more than a dozen years before, Pa had begun to slip into senility. With a sense of foreboding, I picked up the phone and called him.

He answered.

"Hi Pa, how are you?" I said, relieved.

"Good," he said. "I am very good."

He always said that, no matter what his condition.

"Did I interrupt your supper?"

"No, no . . . Edith is here. Heh, heh," he said. "We ordered Chinese food."

Edith was the Jamaican cleaning lady I'd hired to prevent Pa from suffocating in dust balls and dirty shorts. He had fought me for months. Danny said I was wasting my breath, said I should leave Pa to run his life as he always had, but

I couldn't help myself. I was raised to take responsibility whenever it presented itself. I called it filling vacuums.

"I'm just being a good daughter-in-law," I teased.

Danny thought I spoiled Pa.

"Didn't you have enough taking care of your own elderly parents?" He gave me one of his boyish half-smiles to soften the admonishment.

"I guess you must miss them but, Leah, my father's not your parents, okay?"

Pa underscored Danny's theory every time he said, "What do I need a woman to clean? I don't want nobody in my house, touching my things, maybe stealing." But I was adamant. Even Beryl said I should stop wasting my breath but I prevailed, if only so there was one day a week I was assured he was taken care of. Now Pa loved Edith, especially when she stayed late to share supper with him.

The man craved company but would never admit it. He was notorious for refusing to leave his house except for dinner with his kids, attending Sunday brunch at Beryl's, and shopping for his groceries every other day. None of these added up to much exercise. Not even the shopping. The supermarket was only two blocks away and his groceries, a loaf of bread, a tin of halvah, another of canned tuna or packaged smoked meat, did not require any substantial effort to carry. Neither did it constitute a proper diet for a seventy-eight-year-old man with hardened arteries.

Left to his own devices, television had become Pa's most

constant companion. He knew the characters on the reruns of *Gunsmoke* and the history of every hockey player better than he knew Danny.

He did like his Sunday outings. Danny and I would pick him up and take him to Beryl's where, after a brunch of bagel, cream cheese, and lox, Pa sat and watched sports on TV with his two sons. This was the best of times for the three of them, the common ground on which they gathered every Sunday, and the spot where the least amount of friction was generated between Pa and Danny.

Pa had always resented his youngest son. He had not wanted another child; it was enough for him that he had a daughter in Hannah, the eldest, and a son in Beryl, he told me—without thought as to how horrifying the statement sounded.

"But you do love Danny, don't you, Pa?" I had asked. He had shrugged and sucked on a cold pipe.

"Is Danny there?" I asked, feeling foolish.

"No, is he coming?"

"No Pa, I don't think so . . . I just thought, maybe . . . "

"He never comes," Pa said. "Are we going out for supper tonight?" Sometimes, when I managed to guilt Danny into acknowledging that his father was being neglected, we would take Pa to dinner during the week.

"But, Pa, didn't you say you were eating supper with Edith?"

"Ha-ha, yeh, yeh. I meant tomorrow—we'll eat supper tomorrow maybe."

"That's a good idea, Pa. You enjoy your Chinese food, and say hello to Edith for me."

When Danny arrived a few minutes later, I laced into him for disappearing, after making me rush home for supper.

"What are you so upset about?" he shot back. "I wait for you almost every night."

He braced himself for my comeback, but I didn't have one. I was thinking about Pa.

"Hey, don't get so upset," Danny said putting an arm over my shoulder, "I just forgot to drop something off at Gerry's."

"Doesn't matter. It's just . . ." I stopped a minute deciding whether or not to share.

"You just what? Missed me?" Danny was in a good mood.

"I had this feeling."

"Don't tell me you've had another one of your premonitions." He raised his hands and made the sign of the cross as if warding off a vampire. Danny hated my premonitions, but he couldn't completely dismiss them. On a couple of occasions, they had been eerily accurate.

"Pa is getting more and more forgetful and . . . "

"What is this obsession with my father? He's fine. He's just getting old." He shot me his "not now" look and turned to walk away.

Not now. It seemed that was Danny's answer to anything I considered important. In the last year or so, we had stopped talking about the future, as if making plans was futile, as if the future was a place we didn't want to visit. And the present was full of "not now."

Making supper, I couldn't stop thinking about Pa. His forgetfulness had been escalating. It had started out with misplacing unimportant things like a bathmat, the kettle, his watch. When he couldn't find the item fast enough, he would claim it had been stolen. Twice during the last few months, after Danny had dropped by just to say hello, Pa had called to accuse his own son of taking his watch. He was so adamant, I had to drive over, find the watch, and chastise Pa for his accusations. Both times, Pa had stubbornly refused to apologize. At times, I felt like I was the only thing holding Pa and Danny together.

"Why do you always side with him?" Pa had asked.

"Because he's my husband and he's not a thief, Pa. If you keep this up and make me choose between you, who do you think I'm going to choose? My husband or his father?"

"Don't you love me, Leah?" he asked, taking me by surprise. I knew the answer would hurt him so I said, "Pa, I've been your daughter-in-law for almost twenty years. What do you think?" He smiled and I smiled back, only a little ashamed by the success of my ruse.

Six months earlier a failed burglary attempt had given Pa a bad scare. He started locking the deadbolt on his front door from the inside, hiding the key for safety, then forgetting where he had put it. Luckily—or not—we had a spare. Frantic calls came in at all hours of the day and night and then one of us, usually me, would have to go over to find his key and calm Pa down. I even screwed a hook beside the front door and tried to get Pa to hang the key there so it would always be handy. For a while, it cut the calls in half and then things escalated again for no reason. I started to think Pa was using the lost key as a means of getting me to come over.

"What a wife you have," Pa said one night while we were out to dinner. "The smartest thing you ever did was to marry Leah."

It was Danny, though, who ran any errand Pa asked for and took him to the doctors. But no matter how much he did, he received no acknowledgment, no thanks. Danny never said a word. Not to his father. In his late seventies, my father-in-law still held his children in thrall. Hannah, well into her fifties would slip into town from her home in Florida for her yearly visit and warn us not to let on she was there until she was good and ready.

Beryl called her Hannah the Handful. Once a year at family get-togethers, her deep devotion to Absolut vodka usually resulted in the story of how Pa had cast her aside when she was nine to make room for his new baby son, Beryl.

At these dinners, I watched Pa sneak furtive glances

at his family. I saw a lost soul, a man hungry for affection and acknowledgment. Sometimes, sadly, I caught that same look on Danny's face.

Danny and I sat down for dinner but something kept nagging at me.

"You know, Danny, some weeks, if I didn't call him, Pa could drop dead on Monday and we would never know it until the following Sunday."

Danny looked up but continued eating his salad.

"You're all the same—you, Beryl, Hannah—if he doesn't ask for some attention, he doesn't get it."

"It's still more than I ever got," said Danny, pushing the salad bowl away. "And why do you keep after me? He's not your father!"

"That's right, but your family is all the family I've got left, so I care. Besides, he's an old man who's losing it," I said. "Sometimes, I think you'd be more attentive if he was a stranger on the street." Danny was a notoriously soft touch. Panhandlers could smell him at fifty paces.

Danny stiffened his back.

"OK. I'm sorry, Danny, but it seems like everybody just wants Pa to disappear, like he was an inconvenience in our lives or something. That's not right."

"Listen, Leah. What are you suggesting? Putting him in a home? Be practical. How would we convince him? Pa's precious Hannah lives in Lalaland with her young boyfriend and Beryl spends half his week in Toronto and the other half on the golf course, so harping at me who has NOTHING to say about Pa is a waste of time. Besides, even if we all agreed, he never would. You know how Pa loves his house. He'd die if you tried putting him in a home."

Danny was right. All the patterns were locked in and I was just banging my head against the wall. Danny knew better than any of us how stubborn Pa could be. Despite the many little things he did for Pa, it was Beryl who got the love and Hannah the respect. Hadn't Hannah and Beryl made successes of their lives? Look at Beryl's big house and Mercedes; Hannah's ground floor condo facing the ocean off Key Biscayne. Three children each. We had none of that, neither the big house, fancy car, nor any children. According to Pa, all Danny had to show for himself was me.

"Besides, just because you have one of your crazy premonitions doesn't mean we have to drag my father out of the one place where he's happiest."

Pa had done a good job of breeding stubbornness into his children. I had to let it go. Pa was Danny's father and I had to respect that. After so many years of marriage, I wanted to believe I loved Danny as much as the first time I saw him, bending over to kiss his mother good-bye in the convalescent home where we met. There was a tenderness that had left me hungry for inclusion.

Life never turns out the way we plan. One day, we said, we were going to have kids. Danny was going to catch the brass ring and make a ton of money. I was going to finally realize my dream of becoming a world-class potter. I would make beautiful, delicate shapes out of cold clay. Now, 'one day' seemed further away than ever. I sometimes felt as if I were the cold clay, waiting for something to help my life take some meaningful shape.

An hour after dinner, Edith called from her apartment, all worried that she couldn't reach Pa by phone. He had been acting strange all day, she said, and she wanted to check up on him but there was no answer.

"That man is alone too long," she said. "He's losing his good sense. He locked himself in again and couldn't find the key. I had to climb in the kitchen window to get inside that house. I thought he was going to die at my feet from a heart attack. All day he was speaking to me in strange tongues."

"He was probably speaking Russian or Yiddish," I explained. "Thank you for the call, Edith, and for caring. You are very kind."

"You call me back, Miss Leah," said Edith. "I won't sleep til you do."

I called Mrs. Schaeffer, Pa's longtime neighbor and asked if she would go over to check on him, then I walked into the den where Danny was watching sports on his TV. I told him about the call and said that his father needed to be someplace where he could be watched.

"I ask you again—what do you want me to do?"

"Talk to your brother," I said. "Please."

Mrs. Schaeffer called back and said she had seen the TV flickering through the window, but she had to knock several times before there was any answer.

"Leave me alone," Pa had called out in Yiddish, a language he refused to speak with me. He had come to Canada in 1927 and for him, speaking Yiddish was the mark of a greenhorn, a loser.

"He sounded angry," Mrs. Schaeffer said, "so at least we know he's still alive."

I thanked her and marched back into the den, my fists clenching and unclenching. "I'm going over to check on your father," I said.

"He's probably asleep and just forgot to turn off the TV. Don't make something from nothing."

"I won't knock on the door. I have a key."

Danny sat bolt upright.

"You know how afraid he is of robbers coming into his house. Why do you think he keeps locking himself in? If he wakes up while you're trying to get in or sneaking around, you'll give him a heart attack. If he's not dead, Leah, for Chrissake, you'll kill him."

Danny was right. There was no winning action to be employed. I was without options. I made one more stab at trying to convince Danny to talk to his siblings about putting Pa in one of those new assisted-care apartments. He just gave me a cold look like I was nothing more than a blast of wind that blew over him, so I went to bed. I lay there wondering why I couldn't let go of this feeling that this was a test of some kind and that I was failing badly.

Sometime around midnight, Danny woke me. He was sitting on the edge of the bed looking drawn and sad. He said, "You're right. We do need to do something. I'll speak to Beryl on Sunday about what to do with Pa."

I was all ready to smile but a chill ran through me. When I looked up, I thought I saw Pa, standing behind Danny, sucking on his pipe, the smoke curling up toward the ceiling.

"That's good, Danny," I said and rolled over, putting my face in the pillow so he wouldn't see the wetness pooled in the corners of my eyes.

At seven the next morning, I awoke with the image of Pa in my head, still standing as I had seen him the night before. I reached for the phone.

"What are you doing?" asked Danny, his voice muffled with sleep.

"Calling Pa."

"What do you think you're doing? You know he doesn't wake up until at least eight-thirty. Let the poor man get some rest, for God's sake."

What did I think I was doing? And who was I doing it for?

I got up, got dressed, and waited. I called the office to say I'd be late and headed to Pa's around nine. Along the way, the song "Memories" came on the radio and as Barbra Streisand sent her voice into the stratosphere, I began to cry.

I arrived at Pa's duplex and with a shaking hand knocked at the front door. When I heard nothing, I rang the bell. I stood there like a beggar, my head hung down until I remembered Pa's key in my purse. I slipped it in the lock and turned. The door opened a crack, held shut by a chain. Through the narrow opening, I call out, "Pa, Pa?"

There was no answer and I knew: if the chain was still on and Pa was inside, it wasn't good. From some pocket of strength, I put my shoulder to the door and gave it all I had. To my amazement, I ripped the doorjamb off the wall. It dangled from the door as the door swung open.

Across the narrow hallway and the avocado wall-to-wall, I saw a pair of legs. They dangled over the high arm of the living room sofa—two white, blue-veined marble columns. I felt like I was walking underwater. A part of me detached from the heaviness that was settling into my limbs and analyzed the scene.

Pa must have been standing by the door, then stepped back and just as his knees hit the sofa, fallen backwards and died. Although my own legs felt leaden, I managed to maneuver myself to the front of the sofa. And there was Pa, lying on his back, his head turned toward me, his eyes open, as if to say, "Ah, you're here. What took you so long?"

It was all like a dream I had already had—the kind that feels familiar or like a continuation of another dream. It struck me that I had never seen death before, despite losing both my parents years earlier. I had refused to go into their hospital rooms after they'd died or open the lids of their coffins. And here was Pa, for whom I felt compassion but no love; here he was, not only forcing me to face death, but also arranging it so I would be the one to find him. He had summoned me, shaped this moment. Even in death, he was stubborn. I couldn't stop staring back at his glassy gaze. Finally, I went to the linen closet and took down an old Hudson Bay blanket and covered Pa's torso and face, then I forced myself into the hallway where I retrieved the phone and carried it around the corner to the kitchen table.

I called Danny.

"You have to come to Pa's," I said. The lack of emotion in my voice surprised me.

"What's wrong?" he asked.

"He's dead."

The words sounded hollow, like the tail end of an echo.

"Stop joking. That's not funny." There was anger in Danny's voice.

I said nothing. I could almost see Danny, his face impassive, waiting for me to say I was kidding; the dread when he realized it was no joke. I didn't know what else to say without giving in to a rising knot of anger.

"Ohhh, no! I don't believe it," he said. But he did, he just didn't want to go there. But "not now" was no defense against death.

After awhile, I spoke into the silence, "You have to call Beryl."

"I can't. I can't tell Beryl," Danny said. Panic was cutting a sharp edge into his voice. "What would I say? Please, please, you call him."

Bile was churning in my stomach. Ms. Dutiful Daughter. This wasn't my father, I wanted to shout at Danny. Why do I have to call Beryl to tell him Pa is dead? Why do I always have to be the grown-up?

I called Beryl. He told me to stop kidding. When he finally believed there was something wrong, he said he would be there right away. "Pa is probably just in a coma," he said without conviction. " He may only just look dead."

"Maybe," I said. Why should I argue? I was numb. They'd both see for themselves soon enough.

Finally, I called 911 and then the Paperman Funeral Home. Suddenly, my face was wet and my throat ached. It felt like I had a tried to swallow an egg whole. I cried quietly until Danny and Beryl arrived, coming up the front stoop at the same time, as if they had planned to face death together. They came through the front door toward me but no one touched; there were no hugs of consolation, no comforting kisses, only a worried look that kept passing between them. I led them to the couch. They stood waiting for me to remove the blanket as if, even now in death, it was beyond their right to touch their father.

I lifted a corner. Pa's was the face of a man who was angry at having been cheated. His sons stared down as if any moment they expected their father to sit up and reveal the joke. After a moment, I asked who was going to call Hannah in Florida. It was like I had taken my finger out of the dam. A wave of emotion washed over them, followed by a look of genuine terror. They turned to me in unison. After Pa, Hannah frightened the brothers the most.

"You do it, Leah," Beryl said. "She'll take the news better from you. She respects you, Leah, because you're strong. You should be the one to break the news to Hannah."

Defeated, I dialed the number.

Hannah hung up on me three times. First she shrieked. Then she called me a liar. Finally, she sobbed, during which I took the opportunity to suggest that she book a flight to Montréal to come bury her father.

I let out a long breath. All at once, I was a punctured balloon; all the air was seeping out of me. I was there in the little kitchen, but a part of me was M.I.A. What was left was defeated. All my efforts at "fixing" things had been futile. I looked up. Outside the kitchen, in the cramped hallway of their father's duplex, Danny and Beryl stood face-to-face, not looking at one another, but talking in hushed tones. And I realized that something more than Pa had died in that house.

PESACH EN PROVENCE

IN 1989, at the peak of the debate about whether Québec should separate from Canada, I was in a business meeting with some Francophones in Montréal. As the meeting wrapped up, someone made a cutting comment that could be misconstrued as unkind to Anglophones. Everyone laughed and then they remembered I was in the room. All eyes turned my way. The man who had commented shrugged his shoulders and said he was sorry, that he had meant no offence. I said none was taken, but he nonetheless continued, explaining that I couldn't possibly understand what it is like to be afraid that your language will be lost to your children and that your culture will one day disappear. In fact, I said,

I understood perfectly. My mother tongue was Yiddish and it had already been designated a dead language. More to the point, as my parents were Holocaust survivors, I had been raised with the values and mores of a culture that was gone before I was born, leaving me lonely and hungering for something I never had.

In the Alpes-Maritimes, the mountain range lurking behind the Riviera, I rent a cozy and uncluttered apartment from a Danish couple I have never met. I have been coming to Grasse since 1997, at first because I have a second-cousin living here, but now mostly because it is a place where, with a cliff wall rising at my back and a panoramic view plunging to the sea, I can effectively empty myself to make room for the stories I want to write. I come in spring when the air is redolent with thyme, jasmine, and wisteria, Grasse being world famous for its perfumes.

My mother wears Evening in Paris but only on special occasions like Pesach. The midnight blue bottle is the one bright spot on her otherwise drab dresser.

The idea of making a Passover seder first comes to me soon after I arrive in Grasse. I am going through the kitchen cupboards, taking inventory, when I suddenly come across a box of matzo. Two years earlier I had left a half-empty box. I know it's not the same package, but I wonder whether the Danish couple discovered and somehow grew fond of this tasteless, constipating cracker, all because of me.

I am not planning a *real* seder, that would be impossible,

just something to help me through the holiday period, to keep me connected to Montréal despite all the trouble I have gone to by removing myself from there. So I plan a *faux* seder, but for whom? My cousin and her husband will be away, visiting their children in California. Undaunted, I invite my friend Julie, a woman raised by nuns in a Montréal convent and the widow of a real Cossack. The irony is not lost on me. My life is like that, a constant sliding backward and forward along some slippery groove, carved out long before I got here. Wherever I am, a part of me is sliding for a Home somewhere else.

What I know of seders is not informed so much by religious teachings as by the force of family dynamics, the tailoring of the event to various players. That is what now remains of this holiday for me. Before I was even born, World War II consumed most of my family, leaving my brother and me suffering from a deficit of relatives. The few we did have were far-flung; vaguely familiar faces in photographs that arrived in a letter once a year. This deficit was never more obvious than during the holidays, especially Passover. It was just the four of us, five if you count the ghost of the Prophet Elijah.

The kitchen table is moved into the living room because you don't eat dinner in the kitchen on "yontif." We are all dressed in our finest and, despite the lack of company, the table is set with linen, china, and a silver candelabrum.

"Bennick," my mother says to my father who is reveling in the Passover rituals, "do we have to do the whole Hagaddah? The children are hungry."

Because it is a holiday and my mother exhausted from the effort of preparation, my father is able to negotiate for the recounting of one more story. This is the part he is good at, reading out loud to us the story of how we came out of bondage.

My mother was a woman of enormous energy. A week before Passover, there was a frenzy of activity, scrubbing kitchen cupboards to make way for the Passover things. The holidays always caused my mother to become even more highly strung than usual, more likely to snap at my father or brother or me. I remember offering to help once, but my mother took this as an opportunity to remind me what a talent I had for breaking things. Not that we had anything precious, no heirlooms salvaged from previous generations, no treasured pieces passed on with interesting family histories. Our Passover dishes were purchased second-hand in a refugee camp in Germany. And like our family, the set was incomplete.

When I am twelve, I return home from a friend's house to see my mother preparing to store the chometz in our apartment locker.

"Bella's mother says we are supposed to throw out the chometz," I say innocently.

"Bella's mother never buried a child who died from hunger," my mother replies sharply. *"Bella's mother was born here in Canada and never had a hungry day in her life. It's a sin against God to throw away food,"* she says in that tone that suggests the discussion is over.

This is how our family is bound together, as if by the barbed wire from the fences of Auschwitz, a name more familiar to me than Toronto. Growing up, Toronto is the far side of the moon, while Auschwitz could be right outside our door.

For my faux seder, some innovation is required. To make matzo meal, I crush the boxed matzo in the coffee grinder and get the Manischewitz recipe for matzo balls on the Internet. I think about my mother as I make *charoses,* using "Canada" apples grown in France, although I've never seen them at home. I guess if we did grow them in Canada, they'd be called something else, just like French fries are just *frites* in France. In Grasse, I am a Canada apple, but I'm not so sure what I am back in Montréal.

"Bring me the copper pesedikeh plate," my mother calls from the kitchen. *"I will give you a job, if you want to help." I am to grate apples for the charoses while my mother cracks and empties walnuts shells. "You are doing Baileh's job. I always cracked the nuts, Malka mixed it all together with the honey; Ruchmeh would be helping der Mameh and Shaindel would be singing."*

With a few words, my mother conjures up the one-room shteibel *in Chnanow where she lived with her parents and four sisters before The War.*

I am much loved in my family for the turkey and matzo ball soup I make. It's a recipe given to me by my mother while she was in the hospital with the cancer that would kill her at the age of sixty-three. I make the soup every holiday for family gatherings; my family, for the most part, being the one I married into. At twenty, I acquired a pair of sister-in-laws, brother-in-laws, numerous nieces and nephews, three sets of aunts and uncles, and a bonanza of first cousins. When I left the marriage, I kept my dowry of relatives and my position as the best maker of matzo ball soup, that being the part I'm good at.

The seders were invariably held at my brother-in-law's house because, being wealthy, he had the room. The length of the table set for as many as fourteen, all of them immediate family, filled me with happy anticipation. But not having children of my own, the only thing I bring to the evening is the soup. These seders were family gatherings, but without any of the decipherable traditions from my childhood, only a few grudging prayers, laboriously squeaked out by my brother-in-law, once the grandfathers had died. I missed the storytelling, although I had complained about it so bitterly as a young girl. So as much as I treasured the coming together of family, stripped of their ceremony, these seders were often laced with a bittersweet loneliness.

For my faux seder in Provence, I roast a whole chicken stuffed with vegetables and smothered in garlic, a recipe I also find on the Internet. It's too much food and though Julie asks for seconds, I can see I'll have enough for at least three more meals. Too much food is a Passover tradition, I tell her. My mother would lade the table as if all her sisters were coming to dine. It's as if having survived hunger, she had to find ways to reassure herself that we had more food than we needed. As a result, I have inherited an abhorrence of half-filled fridges and sparse meals. I wonder if it's because I am Jewish or because I was raised with a refugee's mentality, or both.

At supper, Julie will ask me if I consider myself a Canadian or a Jew and I tell her that my nationality is Canadian but my soul is Jewish. That satisfies her, but leaves me uneasy, knowing I had not really answered the question.

"When we're gone," my mother repeats like a daily prayer, "you and your brother will only have each other. You are the only ones left of all our family. Remember that. Remember."

In my sleep, sodden with too much food and rosé, I discern a jangling sound that, with a start, I identify as the telephone. I run down the darkened hall.

"Hello?" It's Nancy, my brother's wife calling from

Toronto, where it is only a quarter to six. They're waiting for their seder guests to arrive and I am instantly nostalgic, regretful of being here and not there, in that foreign land called Toronto where my brother, Nancy, and their boys shower me with love when I visit. Nancy, so full of the same kind of energy my mother had, but without the angst and anguish, gives me a rundown of her menu. My mother would have loved her (although I am convinced Nancy would have been nagged into converting). Nancy speaks of having prepared the charoses and having the hard-boiled eggs standing by with the pitcher of salted water, "the salted tears of the Israelites," she reminds me, jokingly. I had forgotten about that.

Nancy is a wonder with her love of puns and the loopy lyrics she makes up, and an ability to invent new traditions when she cannot draw on the old. One Passover seder when the boys were young, she held a matzo board to her face and created Matzo Man. She sang it to the tune of the Village Peoples' "Macho Man." It became a tradition for a while.

Now I crawl back into my narrow Provençal bed, groggy with half-formed thoughts and the weight of too much food and drink. Throughout the day, my mother had been shadowing me as I washed the floors of the apartment and prepared my faux seder. She is back now, hovering on the edge of my consciousness, intruding on my attempts to retrieve sleep. I wonder what she's trying to tell me, what I was thinking to have made so much food, why I found it important to cook all day for just Julie and me. I could easily have done something simple. But then, I think while drifting off, it would not have been a Passover seder; it would have just been a friend coming over for dinner. Where's the memory in that?

ACKNOWLEDGMENTS

The older you get, the more people there are to thank. I have been blessed with friends and family and angels whose generosity of spirit all along the way has helped me beyond measure. I am grateful to my mentors, two outstanding women—Lena Allen-Shore and Twinkle Rudberg—from whom I learned that nothing is impossible when you have passion, dedication, and tenacity. I can add to that list the remarkable Margie Wolfe who heard something she liked and was patient enough for me to figure out what it was. For Marsha Berman, Florence Millman, David Conrod, Georgi Beal, Matthew Cope, Roz Luks and Linda Fox, I thank you for your support, fierce belief in me and endless encouragement. I was privileged to have teachers who freely shared their knowledge and experiences—Ann Diamond,

Elaine Kalman Naves, Joel Yanofsky, Ami Sands Brodoff and Wayson Choy. Most important of all, I thank my remarkably talented writing group, MontrealWrites. Elizabeth Ulin, Maggie Kathwaroon, Sarah Lolley, Paul Robichaud and lately, Derek Webster, your passion, eagle-eyes and clear-thinking are woven into every story you have critiqued over the last three years. Hopefully, that made the job of my editor and guardian angel, Carolyn Jackson, a little easier. And finally, I thank Axel Augustin for confirming my faith in the universe.